ALIEN PERIL

It reared up out of the turf, a living cylinder, thick and flexible like an oversized worm. Cord saw that it was covered with a thick segmented shell, like plates of armor. It was eyeless, with a spray of thin tendrils sprouting from the front of its head. And on the underside of the head was a wide gaping mouth, surrounded by long, sturdy tentacles, each with a sharp, barbed hook at the end.

The creature slid swiftly forward in an oozing slither, disturbingly silent. One of the tentacles around the repulsive mouth struck out like a snake. Lamprey raised the laser rifle and took aim. The beam struck dead center. But nothing happened. . . .

EXILES OF COLSEC

DOUGLAS HILL

BANTAM BOOKS
TORONTO · NEW YORK · LONDON · SYDNEY · AUCKLAND

FOR J.G.
*in rueful acknowledgment
of the First Law*

RL 7, IL age 12 and up

EXILES OF COLSEC
A Bantam Spectra Book / June 1986

ISBN 0–553–25785–4

Published simultaneously in the United States and Canada

Bantam Books are published by Bantam Books, Inc. Its trademark, consisting of the words ''Bantam Books'' and the por-
trayal of a rooster, is Registered in U.S. Patent and Trademark
Office and in other countries. Marca Registrada. Bantam
Books, Inc., 666 Fifth Avenue, New York, New York 10103.

PRINTED IN THE UNITED STATES OF AMERICA

O   0 9 8 7 6 5 4 3 2 1

Contents

1

Dream and Nightmare

The broad chamber, with walls and low ceiling of blank, colourless metal, lay in shadow and silence. Only the muted glow from a computer screen, set into one wall of the area, interrupted the darkness. But nothing interrupted the stillness.

It was the empty, gloomy stillness of a long-forgotten tomb. And it was made all the more tomb-like by the twelve containers fastened solidly to the metal floor in the centre of the area.

In shape they were like caskets, or large coffins, made of sturdy condensed plastic. But inside, they were softly padded—the padding moulded to the individual shapes of the twelve bodies that lay within. Youthful human bodies, as silent and still as everything else in the area, eyes closed, with no sign of heartbeat or breathing.

But in the sides of the containers, behind the padding, were complex devices that worked to nourish, to preserve and support life. Through the padding a host of needles reached out to thrust deeply beneath the skin of the bodies. Other parts of the skin were covered with the electrodes of monitors and scanners. And so the bodies were healthy and alive.

Now and then a group of muscles might ripple and flex uncannily, but the movement was caused by a gentle shock from an electrode, to maintain muscle tone and fitness. The minds within the bodies felt no movement. The minds were in a sleep that went beyond sleep, a coma of life in suspension.

Yet within the deepest reaches of those minds, the dreams lived.

Stormy, chaotic dreams, most of them, of grim and ruined landscapes, of misery and hardship—but also of laughter and crashing music and wild, high-speed excitement. In two of the young minds, the dreams centred on a sprawling urban area of crumbling buildings and filthy, broken streets, an area that armed and armoured Civil Defenders entered only in hover-tanks. It was a place populated by human refuse—the thugs and the druggies, the twisted and the insane, the hopeless and the defeated. It was a place called Limbo.

But among the outcasts of that place roamed other groups—packs of young people, wearing strange garb, finding their excitement in acts of petty crime and violence: the free Streeters of Limbo, homeless but not helpless, defiantly rejecting the grey, dull, ordered world around them.

In another casket, a similar dream—of wild, violent, strangely decorated youths turning their backs on the regulated ordinary world. But this was a dream of chill and gloom and damp, in endless underground passages, called the Bunkers—rat-warrens beneath the ruins of a once-magnificent capital city. There the youths made their free lawless domain, where even the most coldly determined squads of Civil Defenders could not pursue them.

But in a different casket, a different dream. Images tinged with melancholy beauty—of an unending sweep of dusty plain, of high hot summer skies, of the eye-searing winter sun on fresh snowfields. And mingled with these images, the memory of isolation, of bone-twisting cold, of the clench of hunger.

Oddly, in among the images that lived in that one dreamer, there came fragmented glimpses of other scenes. Wild pursuits through crumbling city streets, noisy charges through dark twisting tunnels. Scenes filled with the shadowy forms of young people, weirdly dressed, with strange distorted faces. . . .

Then again, another mind in another casket had its own individual dream. This one recalled a land of storm-clouded skies and lancing rain, of steep brush-covered mountain slopes and wide lakes of black and pitiless water. But to the dreamer it was a land of beauty and delight, made into a place of joy by the presence of a red-bearded giant wearing skins and furs and cloth with a colourful criss-cross pattern— the beloved uncle, who had raised the young dreamer in that wild land and taught him all its ways.

The dream recalled the breathless stalking of vast herds of red deer; the warmth of a small stone hut and a dancing fire that kept the icy wind at bay; occasional nights among other wild folk in skins and furs, the graceful leaping dances, the soul-saddening music, the drinking and tale-telling and competitive tests of strength. And the young dreamer relived his own part in those tests, when he was grown to a stocky bulk of solid muscle, and set a gleam of pride in the uncle's eyes.

But then the dream shifted, from happiness to horror. The fall that had injured the uncle—and the young dreamer slinging the huge groaning body over his powerful shoulders and walking forty kilometres to the nearest civilized place of streets and houses, to seek help. Help that was refused, because the young one had none of the necessary stuff called money.

Then the death of the beloved uncle, in raging agony, and the red fury that bloomed within the young man, amid grief and loss and thunderous hate. That fury had set out to smash the clinic that had turned the dying uncle away—and it had needed half a dozen club-wielding Civil Defenders to subdue it.

The dream then remembered days of drugged mindlessness in a cage, the cloudy awareness of a five-minute trial, and the judgment: transportation, for life, to the prison colony of Antarctica, as befell all young offenders against the civil order.

So that dream came to its end, as it had many times before. But before it might begin again, as it also had continuously done, like an endless loop of video tape, something wholly unusual stopped it.

Alone among all the sleepers in the twelve caskets, in that dim, metal-walled chamber, that dreamer awoke.

*   *   *

His body was filled with a vibrating throb of pain, and his mind was filled with nothingness. Empty-eyed, he watched needles and electrodes slide back into the padded sides of the casket. Empty-eyed, he stared down at his body—the slightly freckled skin, the solidity of mounded muscle—and did not recognize it. Slowly he closed his eyes, as if seeking to return to the dream.

But his eyes jerked open again as another needle probed out from the padding, into his skin. The injection seemed to flow through his every cell, in a wave of cool soothingness. The pain receded—and with it went the clouds in his mind.

He remembered. He was Cord MaKiy, sixteen years old, and a Highlander, one of the wanderers of a harsh and beautiful land too bleak and poor and remote to interest the rulers of the rest of the world. And, he remembered, he was no longer in that land.

He clamped his eyes shut again, but tears seeped through his eyelids as the memories relentlessly formed. The beloved uncle was dead, the Highlands lost to him forever. And he, Cord MaKiy, was a criminal, condemned forever to the Antarctic prison.

But then his jaw tightened, and muscles leaped and bunched in his arms as he clenched his fists. If he was awake, he thought, they must be arriving. And he would not arrive tear-stained and whimpering like a child.

He opened his eyes once more, and felt a jolt of surprise. The top of the casket had raised itself, on silent hinges. He saw a blank dimness above him, a slightly curved ceiling of colourless metal. Slowly he sat up, shivering slightly in the thin, cool air. He was not aware that, until some moments before, there had been neither air nor warmth in that metal-walled chamber.

At his feet he saw a bundle of muddy-brown clothing—strange to him, though commonplace in the ordinary world. Plain tunic and trousers, sturdy boots. Automatically he pulled on the clothes, ran fingers through his tangle of auburn hair, then clambered from the casket. He realized that his body was moving normally, yet somehow he felt slow and weary, and wondered for a moment how long he had been unconscious in the casket.

And why, he asked himself, should they send us this way, to Antarctica? It can't be that far. . . .

But he knew he was not familiar with many of the ways of the civilized world. So he let the question go, trying to ignore the twist of unease within him.

He stared around blankly at the other eleven caskets, closed and silent. Then his eye was caught by a sudden brightness across the area. Sharply defined golden letters had appeared on the screen of the computer.

He moved towards it. He had learned something of reading and writing from his uncle, but even so he read the letters slowly, with puzzlement.

THIS IS A GUIDANCE AND DATA STOR-AGE COMPUTER SHUTTLE-FORM 181-QX9 VOICE PROJECTIVE AND VOICE ACTIVATED SPEAK ALOUD TO BEGIN COMMUNICATION

Cord understood only a little of it, but grasped the idea that he should say something.

"Uh . . . what do I say?" He felt a little foolish,

and his voice croaked from lack of use. But it did not seem to matter.

"Thank you for activating me." The computer's voice was soft and human, but totally without emotion. "I am known as GUIDE. I am here to provide information and to answer your questions."

Cord blinked, unable to think for a moment. "Good," he said at last. "You can... you can tell me if we've got to Antarctica, now."

"Antarctica is on Earth," the soft voice of GUIDE told him. "You are not on Earth."

For all their quiet tone, the words struck Cord like hammers. His legs felt weak, his flesh cold, his mind reeling. It wasn't true, he thought numbly. How could it be true? It was a lie—a joke—maybe a form of mind-bending torture, a cruel invention of the Civil Defenders....

But the computer was going on, doing its duty, providing information.

"You and the others are inside an orbital shuttle, which is being carried by a space freighter, en route to a Colonization Section base in the Procyon planets. The shuttle will be automatically released when the freighter passes near a planet named Klydor, after a flight of four months. We are now approaching Klydor, and have left translight and re-entered normal space. After release, the shuttle is programmed to land on Klydor, where you and the others will seek to establish a new human colony."

Even in his daze, Cord understood much of that. Some kind of spaceship, carried by another spaceship, to be dropped off on some planet....

Disbelieving horror brought the sudden sourness of nausea into his mouth. It couldn't be. . . . The frozen wastes of Antarctica would have been bad enough—but another planet? Earth some unimaginable, unbridgeable distance away, lost to him forever, as he was flung unconscious across space, to some unknown alien world. . . . Flung by ColSec. . . .

Deep within him, behind the fear and horror and shock, a small red flame began to burn—a flame of wild, barbaric anger. The flame did not grow or spread, but it had been ignited, and it would not fade or die. It was born of hatred—for ColSec, Colonization Section, one part of the vast organization that gripped the entire Earth in its demanding, oppressive control.

Trying to fight the numbing shock, Cord forced his mouth to form words. "When?" he croaked. "When do we get there?"

"That cannot be computed," said the soft voice of GUIDE. "There is a malfunction. The shuttle is unable to disengage."

For a moment Cord felt he would go insane. There was too much horror, there were too many sudden unbelievable facts that he barely understood, yet that filled him with raw and screaming fear. He stood rooted, covered in a sudden drenching sweat, trembling and unseeing. Yet, as if hypnotized, he heard every soft word as the computer went on.

"The humans in the shuttle have two alternative courses of action. I am not programmed to make human decisions. You have been awakened, to decide."

2

The Choice

Somehow the word "decide" rolled back some of the clouds of shock from Cord's mind. Out of the depths of memory he heard his uncle's deep voice, words that he had heard many times. "In this land we are our own masters, laddie," the uncle would say. "We live as we will, walk where we please. We decide for ourselves."

The memory steadied Cord, and again he found his voice. "Why choose *me*?"

"The psychological profiles of all of you are in my data banks," GUIDE told him. "Yours has the necessary qualities to make the decision."

Cord took a deep breath. He was not sure what a psychological profile was, but he was unwilling to appear weak or afraid, even to a computer. "What is it, then? What must I decide?"

And in that soft unperturbed voice, the computer told him.

The shuttle-craft was attached to the outside of

the freighter, to be automatically released at the right time. But the release mechanism had gone wrong, and the shuttle was unable to detach itself so that it could head for the planet Klydor. One course of action, then, would be for Cord and the others to remain where they were, and hope to cross the path of another human spacecraft, while the freighter went on towards its destination—which it would reach in a further six months.

But if they did *not* intersect with another ship, GUIDE said, then when the freighter finally reached its goal the young people would no longer be alive.

"The caskets were not designed for a voyage of such length," GUIDE explained. "The nutrients and other elements that have kept you alive, for the past four months of suspended animation, have been nearly used up. And the shuttle's power source could not take over the life support systems for that length of time."

Cord shook his head numbly, again grasping only the general meaning. If they stayed where they were, in space, they would soon die.

"What's the other choice?" he asked.

GUIDE told him. The simple controlling pro-gramme that kept the freighter on its course could be over-ridden, through a link-up with GUIDE. The entire freighter, with the shuttle attached, could be made to divert to Klydor.

"That's it, then!" Cord said. But then his face fell. "Except I don't know how to...override...what it was you said."

"That is not the problem," GUIDE said. "The problem is that space freighters are not constructed for planetary landings."

Freighters were loaded and unloaded from orbit, in space, GUIDE explained. If this freighter were diverted, towards Klydor, it would not land. It would burn up in the atmosphere, or crash.

Cord stared at the quiet glow of the screen, again feeling himself beginning to shake. "You're . . . you're saying it's a choice between two different ways of *dying*!"

"That cannot be computed," GUIDE told him softly. "There are many random factors. In either case, there is a chance that at least some of you might survive. But chance is not computable with accuracy."

Cord's mind felt battered. For a desperate moment he wanted to be back in his casket, safely asleep and in his dream. Or was all this another dream, a nightmare, from which he would waken to find himself in the Antarctic prison colony? But he shook himself, fighting the urge to escape into childishness, or madness.

"You should wake the others," he told GUIDE. "They should have a say in how they are to die."

"Psychological profiles say that the decision would not then be made," GUIDE replied. "It must be made by only one. Please inform me of your decision."

Cord's vision blurred as he fought his inner battle, to make sense of what he had been told, what he had to do. For several moments the area was again still and silent, as that battle went on. And then a strange clear thought entered Cord's mind.

The freighter belonged to ColSec, carrying some kind of cargo to some other distant, colonized planet. If Cord and the others remained where they were, and died before the freighter reached its goal, ColSec would probably not blink an eye at the loss of twelve lives.

But if the freighter crashed on Klydor, ColSec would lose something that mattered. It would lose two valuable spacecraft, and the freighter's cargo.

If I have to die, Cord thought fiercely, I want ColSec to suffer a little too.

And anyway, a further thought came, I would die properly, a quick and blazing death, on my feet rather than like a sleeping baby in a casket. The uncle would approve of that.

"We'll take the freighter to Klydor," he said at last, his voice low and hoarse. "If you can show me how."

At once streams of figures and symbols began to appear on GUIDE's screen. And the computer's voice seemed almost gentle.

"There is no need," GUIDE said. "I have begun the awakening of another of your number, who can programme the override."

Cord turned slowly. A casket next to his own had begun to open. The occupant was hidden from him by the raised lid, but Cord knew what that person would be going through. The pain, the emptiness of mind, the slow return to awareness, and to fear. . . .

But in a shorter time than Cord would have imagined, the occupant of that casket emerged, wearing muddy-brown trousers and tunic like those supplied to Cord. And despite the shock that still clawed at his mind, after what he had learned from GUIDE, his first reaction was a childish feeling of chagrin—because she was a centimetre or two taller than he was.

For all his pride in his powerfully muscled, athletic body, Cord had always been self-conscious about his height. He was not tall, and the breadth and solidity of him made him look even shorter. But at least the girl didn't seem interested in his appearance, or in him at all. She was staring, wide-eyed, around the chamber, and especially at the computer screen.

Cord saw that she was slim and tanned, with a rich gleam in her short, tawny-blonde hair. Her face was unremarkable, even plain, but made nearly pretty by her large grey eyes, and by the shaky smile that she at last turned towards Cord.

"I'm Samella Connel," she said. "Have we arrived?"

"Cord MaKiy," Cord said, trying to keep his voice steady. "I have to tell you, we're not at Antarctica. We're...."

"I know," the girl cut in, astonishingly. "We've been in suspended animation, going through translight to some planet."

Cord's mouth dropped open. "You know? How...?"

Samella shrugged. Her shakiness seemed to be fading rapidly. "The ColSec people talked, and I listened. They didn't seem to notice, or care." Her gaze drifted past Cord, towards the jumble of data on the computer screen. "What's going on? Why are you and I awake, and not the others?"

"I...it's...." Cord stumbled. Then he waved a

hand helplessly at the computer. "This machine can tell you better than me. It's called GUIDE."

And the soft expressionless voice of GUIDE told Samella what was happening.

As it spoke, her eyes filmed over with tears, and she began to tremble. "Then we've come all this way to die?" she said at last, her voice faltering.

"That cannot be computed," GUIDE said.

"Is there nothing we can do," Samella asked, "to free the shuttle? A manual release? Repairs?"

"You cannot leave this area," GUIDE said. "There is no equipment on board for humans to enter vacuum."

Samella sagged, and turned blindly towards Cord. For a moment she stared unseeingly at him, and he watched silently as she fought her own inner battle against shock and mind-twisting panic. With relief and growing respect, he saw in a moment that her trembling was ceasing, her eyes re-focusing. She's tough, he thought. And just as well.

"I'm glad it wasn't me who had to choose," Samella said to Cord at last, her voice firmer now.

"I wish it hadn't been me," Cord said truthfully. "I suppose . . . I chose to crash on the planet just so ColSec would lose something too."

For an instant there was a glint of approval in Samella's grey eyes, a small reflection of the flame of hatred that still burned within Cord. "I'm glad of that, too," she said. Then she took a deep breath. "I'll get on with the re-programme."

Cord watched, uncomprehending but impressed, as her slim fingers began to flash over the computer keys. After several minutes, she stepped back with a small sigh, as the screen cleared itself.

"It's done," she said, half to herself. "Klydor, here we come." Then she looked thoughtfully at the computer. "GUIDE, can you predict our chances of surviving the crash?"

"That cannot be computed," GUIDE said again.

Samella frowned slightly. "Random factors? But you'll know our velocity and angle of impact and so on. Do you know about the planet's surface?"

"Details of the planet's features are in my data banks," GUIDE said.

"So," Samella asked, "what kind of terrain will we come down on?"

"The freighter will descend," GUIDE replied, "at a flat angle, to minimize impact, into an area of dense vegetation."

"That's something," Samella said, her eyes brightening. "Then what are the random factors?"

"There are several. How the atmosphere will affect the freighter, since its hull lacks heat-shielding. Whether the freighter will roll, placing the shuttle beneath it when it crashes. Whether the shuttle's hull will resist an impact of unknown force. Whether..."

"All right," Samella broke in. "Now set accuracy aside, and give an *estimate* of survival probability."

The words sounded oddly formal, and Cord guessed that it was some kind of standard instruction to a computer. He wasn't sure he really wanted to know the answer, but he listened with wary interest.

"Understood," GUIDE said calmly. "Chances of survival for all humans on the shuttle, 12 to 15 percent."

"As low as that," Samella whispered.

"Chances of survival for eleven of twelve humans," GUIDE went on, "17 to 20 percent. For ten of twelve, 20 to 26 percent. For..."

The quiet voice continued to roll out the dismal figures. And yet the percentages steadily rose, and a vague feeling of hope stirred within Cord.

"Chances for five of twelve," GUIDE was saying, "48 to 52 percent. Chances...."

"That's enough," Samella broke in. She glanced wanly at Cord. "There's probably a *very* good chance that one person would survive. But I wouldn't want to be that person, alone on an alien world."

Cord wasn't sure he agreed—but then he was used to a lonely life in a hostile environment. "You'd be alive," he pointed out. "And you'd have GUIDE."

"Chances of GUIDE computer surviving the crash intact," the computer put in, "40 to 43 percent."

Cord subsided, feeling oddly troubled that the computer could so coolly predict its own destruction. Of course it was only a machine, but....

"Anyway," Samella was saying, "it's all statistics. There *are* too many random factors. Those figures are really saying that *some* of us may have a chance—but not much of one."

Cord nodded, swallowing hard. If this girl could be so cool, in the face of approaching death, he was determined to do the same.

"What was all that," he asked as calmly as he could, "about the freighter and the...atmosphere?"

"Freighter ships don't ever leave deep space," Samella explained, "so they don't have heat shields, like the shuttle has. When this freighter hits the

planet's atmosphere, it'll heat up, and maybe burn...."
Her mouth trembled for a moment before she regained
control. "And I don't know if the shuttle's heat
shields could handle that. Or how long it would be
before the heat affected the freighter's space-drive."

Cord blinked, mystified. "How would it affect
it?"

To his amazement, he saw a small wry smile tug
at the corners of Samella's mouth. "It could make
the drive explode. And then we wouldn't crash.
We'd just make a nice bright light in the sky over
Klydor."

3

World of ColSec

The long moment of silence that followed was broken at last by the calm voice of GUIDE. "The freighter will enter the planet's outer atmosphere," it said, "in one hour, eight minutes and forty-three seconds."

The two young people looked at each other.

"I suppose we could get into the caskets just before entry," Samella said. "It might improve our chances." She gave Cord another of her crooked half-smiles. "I'm glad you're not turning into a blubbering wreck."

To his surprise, Cord found himself smiling back at her. He was also surprised to realize that he had begun to feel calmer, almost fatalistic, about what was to happen in little more than an hour. And with that feeling came gratitude, for he knew that his calmness owed much to the quiet control of the slim girl who had joined him.

"If you think about it," he said slowly, "we

might not have had much of a chance anyway, on an alien planet, even if we had landed safely."

Samella nodded. "Could be. The ColSec people said it's pretty wild."

"I wish I could have heard some of what they said," Cord replied angrily. "I feel so . . . *ignorant!*"

"Do you?" Samella looked interested, and Cord found himself explaining by telling her about himself.

He began haltingly, but she was an ideal listener, silent, involved, absorbed. So his shyness eased, and he became almost eloquent as he described the wonders of the remote land where he had grown up, all the excitement and danger and happiness of his life with the beloved uncle.

And finally he brought the story to its sombre climax, with the death of the uncle, and the wild explosion of vengeful violence that had branded him a criminal, and brought him at last into the clutches of ColSec.

Samella was silent for a while when he finished speaking, looking at him with vast empty distances and sadnesses in her eyes. But then she blinked and came back to the present.

"And I always thought," she said, half to herself, "that the Highland barbarians were just a story— made up by one of my fathers."

Cord had bristled slightly at being called a barbarian, but her final words made him stare. "*One* of your fathers?"

She grinned. "I lived in a communal family. Lots of adults, lots of kids, no one knowing or caring who was whose, because we all belonged to each other." The grin faded into bleakness. "Or I thought we did."

"Tell me," Cord said gently. "It's your turn."

Samella shrugged, took a deep breath, and began.

She had been born, she said, in the flat dust-bowl region to the north of the American Segment. A place once called Minnesota, or Manitoba—no one was sure which. The communal family—nearly thirty of them—lived their jumbled lives together in a huge tumble-down farmhouse, totally isolated in the midst of the arid plain.

It was a wretched life of bitter poverty, scratching for survival in the almost lifeless soil. Yet there was great happiness, too, Samella said—the freedom, the warmth of love and belonging. Or so, through her childhood, it had seemed.

"What happened?" Cord asked quietly.

Samella looked at the floor, her eyes filling with tears. "They sold me."

Cord stared, aghast, as she went on. A dealer had come to the farm, a dealer in human beings—offering money to anyone who would sign a contract that would make him or her an "indentured worker," nearly a slave. Whoever owned the contract could require the worker to labour for almost no pay, out of which the worker could try—more or less hopelessly—to repay the original sum of money and regain his or her freedom.

That had been three years earlier, when Samella was thirteen. Her family had had a bitter winter of near-starvation, and the money had been too tempting. To save the rest of them, they sacrificed her.

In her near-slavery she had been re-sold by the

dealer to a company in a giant urban complex known as Minneapolis. There she had been trained in ultramodern electronics and computers. And she had shown an amazing natural aptitutde, swiftly becoming expert. Too swiftly, for her own good.

"Some of the other indents were jealous of me," she explained. "So they got together and accused me of stealing. I wouldn't have known how—or what to do with anything stolen. But they were believed. I was tried and convicted—and sent to ColSec."

Cord could taste her bitter pain as if it were his own. "And then you found out you weren't going to Antarctica," he said. "Did everyone know that but me?"

"No," Samella assured him. "Most of the younger prisoners had a history of street crime and violence, so they were kept drugged, like you were. But they didn't waste drugs on me. And they didn't care what they said in front of me. They knew I wouldn't be telling anyone."

"So the world doesn't know what ColSec has done with us," Cord said.

"If they know," Samella replied, "they don't care. But ColSec doesn't tell the world just how far they've reached into space to create colonies. And they don't advertise the fact that they send *kids* out. Young criminals—like us." Her mouth twisted. "They reckon that we're adaptable enough to handle strange new things. But mainly, we're *expendable*. If we get a colony going, then ColSec can come along and claim it. If we get killed off somehow—ColSec just shrugs and sends some more. There are always plenty more."

"How can they get away with it?" Cord burst out.

Samella looked at him wryly. "You really *don't* know much about the world, do you?"

Cord glowered, but he knew she was right. The uncle had known a lot about the world, but rarely spoke of it. So Cord knew only vaguely about the Virus Decades, a century before, that had wiped out much of Europe and Asia and eastern America. And he had only a dim idea of the Organization, formed by rich and powerful people, that had taken charge of the wreckage of human civilization, and dragged the world out of its new Dark Age.

But at least Cord knew how the Organization now ruled the world, through its huge, almost self-governing sections. AgriSec, MediaSec, EnergSec and more. And ColSec.

Colonization Section, with its own spacefleet operating out of Antarctica, where the prison colony serviced the spaceport. ColSec, searching non-stop for resources and raw materials, beyond the damaged and depleted Earth.

And of course Cord knew how ColSec could get away with their ruthless colonization methods. Simply because it was part of the Organization, which held the whole world in its steely, repressive grip.

The people of the Organization's world were regimented into flat, grey, empty lives, almost like robots. Wherever they lived, they dressed the same, spoke the same language, lived the same way—obeyed the same laws, that were enforced by the harsh cruelties of the Civil Defenders. Under those laws, people lived in fearful obedience, not daring to question or resist, not daring even to be different.

Many times, Cord remembered, his uncle had mourned the loss of so many of the old Highland ways—even the unique speech patterns. So the world of the Organization had some effect even on the most remote areas, the poor and empty regions that were usually left alone because they were of no use.

Samella's voice broke into these swarming thoughts. "I suppose I didn't know much, either, when I was on the prairies. But at least you and I had a taste of freedom, which is more than most people get. And it could have been worse. We could have grown up in the inner cities."

When Cord looked at her questioningly, she continued.

"In some of the oldest cities, where the centres are really poor and ruined, there are gangs of kids. They live wild and rough, like—outcasts, or rebels. They're the biggest problem that the Civil Defenders have got." She smiled her crooked smile. "I don't suppose they're *all* as bad as people say—but they give the CeeDees a hard time."

"I knew none of this," Cord said blankly.

"Neither did I, once," Samella said. "The CeeDees keep it quiet, so people don't get the idea that it's possible to fight back. But some of the biggest gangs get on the TV news now and then. Like the Streeters, who just about *own* the centre of the Chicago-Detroit complex—called Limbo. And in your part of the world, there are tunnels and things underneath old London, called the Bunkers, full of kids who are *really* wild." She gestured towards the ten silent caskets nearby. "Some of them, in there, will be kids like that. They might not be nice company, even if we make it to Klydor."

Cord half-smiled, his mind whirling with all the new information. It felt strange, to have found out so much when his life might be about to end. But it was good to know—good to think about the small armies of wild kids, on Earth, who would still be going on with their defiance of the Organization that had created ColSec. . . .

Samella's voice brought him out of his thoughts. "It's funny," she was saying, "but in the casket, some of the time, I was dreaming about those other kids. I remember seeing Limbo, and the Bunkers—and what must have been the Highlands, from what you've said. I saw them all in detail. Yet I've never *really* seen them. Not even on the TV, because even when the gangs get mentioned, MediaSec won't allow *pictures* of them. Might give people ideas. Did you have strange dreams like that, Cord?"

"No," Cord said. "I dreamed about the Highlands, just familiar things. Maybe. . . ."

But then the soft voice of GUIDE interrupted.

"The freighter will enter atmosphere in three minutes," it said. "Seven minutes to impact."

Cord froze, and saw Samella flinch and turn pale. Almost without knowing it, their hands reached out to one another, gripped tight.

"We'd better get into the caskets," Samella said shakily.

Their hands slid apart as they moved towards the caskets, and Samella tried hard to manage one of her wry smiles.

"Nice to have met you, Cord MaKiy."

"I'm glad you were here, Samella," Cord said simply.

For a few seconds they looked solemnly at each other. Then around them they heard a throbbing bass hum, which began to swell and rise. Beneath their feet the metal floor suddenly jerked and heaved, as if some monstrous force had grasped the shuttle and shaken it.

Samella staggered and almost fell. But Cord flung out a powerful arm, scooped her up and dropped her into her casket. As the lid began to lower over her, he made his way to his own casket, though the floor was now juddering and shaking as if the monstrous force was trying to batter its way in.

He climbed into the casket, feeling the padding gather round his body, watching the lid come down like the final closing of a coffin.

"One minute to impact," said the soft voice of GUIDE. But there was no one to hear it.

Yet the casket could not muffle the terrible sounds of the freighter's plunge through the planet's atmosphere. Even muffled, it was a grating, piercing howl, like the screaming of a thousand beasts in agony. Cord's vision blurred, and blood seeped from his nostrils as a crushing pressure clamped down on him. He could hardly breathe, though the casket had its own oxygen supply.

Then, even through the monstrous sound of the ship's howling dive, he heard the agonized ripping of metal strained beyond its limits. The shuttle jolted and heaved, rearing back, twisting, bucking. Cord cried out, but could not hear himself over the still-rising howl, the rending shriek of torn metal. His lungs were bursting, his eyes seemed filled with blood, his very bones seemed to be crumbling under the monstrous pressure.

Yet in the depths of his mind, a silent, defiant yell shaped itself, born not of terror but of a barbarian's rage and pain.

Go on! Finish it! Get it done!

As if in response, he felt an unbelievable hammer blow against the underside of the shuttle, driving Cord deep into the casket's padding, every cell of his body screaming. He heard more metal crackling and collapsing—and felt the sturdy bolts that held the casket to the floor shear and rip away.

Again he tried to cry out as the casket was flung upwards, whirling and spinning like a dry leaf in a gale. He tried to brace himself for the final impact. But he did not feel it when it came.

4

Strangers

He came awake with a scream in his throat.

Shocked by the sound, he lay still with his eyes squeezed shut, willing himself not to scream again. Slowly, his mind explored the sensations of his body.

He was still grasped by the casket's padded interior, almost painfully. The air was foul and thick, and his chest ached with the effort of breathing. His heart pounded heavily, sweat oozed from his pores, and there was the rusty-metal taste of blood in his mouth. And every centimetre of his flesh felt as if he had been endlessly beaten with giant clubs.

Yet each of those sensations came to him through a filter of the purest joy—a joy that arose from four words, which he tried to speak aloud through blood-smeared lips.

"I am not dead."

But breathing was growing more and more difficult. The oxygen supply inside the casket must have been damaged. He raised his arms, which for all their bulge of hard muscle felt weak as wet paper, and pushed upwards against the lid. It did not move.

An edge of panic crept into his mind, and with it came anger—that he might have survived the crash only to suffocate within the casket. The anger poured adrenalin through his battered body, and he heaved furiously up against the lid.

With a grinding wrench, it fell away, and cool air rushed in like a tonic. Slowly, ignoring the throb of bruises, Cord climbed out of the casket.

Around him was chaos and horror.

One entire end of the chamber, the shuttle's interior, was now a shambles of crumpled and splintered metal, bulging inwards, bristling with ragged edges, the floor beneath it littered with shards and fragments. A narrow hatchway at that end, which would have led into an adjoining area, had been burst open—and so had another doorway, some kind of airlock, in one side of the shuttle. Through them both Cord could feel the inward drift of cool, damp air.

But he took in those details in a swift glance, because his appalled gaze was drawn to what remained of the caskets.

They had all been torn free from the floor, and had been flung in a huddled heap against the far wall, that held the console of GUIDE. The computer's screen was now smashed, and GUIDE was deathly silent. As were the caskets.

Cord saw that his own casket had somehow landed rightside up, partly on top of the others. At the bottom of that heap, he saw that at least five caskets were crushed and shattered, and that a spreading pool of blood was forming under all five.

Sickened, he looked elsewhere. Six caskets seemed mostly intact, but he had no way of knowing which was Samella's. He stumbled forward to the nearest one, hesitated, then wrenched the lid away.

Not Samella. A boy about his own age, with a cloud of thick curly hair—and quite dead. A long splinter of metal, no doubt hurled from the front of the chamber as the wall had crumpled inwards, had driven through the side of the casket and speared into the side of the boy's head.

Grimly, Cord moved away. At least he and the others wouldn't have felt a thing, he thought. Then he reached for the lid of the next casket.

Samella lay within it. Her face, like Cord's, was sweat-streaked and blood-smeared, with a larger trickle of blood from where she had bitten her lower lip. She looked peaceful, somehow very young, and entirely motionless.

Cord felt a choking sensation in his throat, his eyes stinging, as he looked at her. But then he rubbed his eyes and looked again. It was true. Her lips had parted slightly, and her tunic had lifted with an intake of breath. And Cord yelled aloud.

"Samella!"

She did not move. But behind him, a soft expressionless voice replied.

"Thank you for re-activating me."

Cord's head jerked around as if he had been slapped. "GUIDE! You're alive too!"

"That does not compute," GUIDE replied calmly. "My casing is broken and my ship guidance system has been destroyed. But many of my memory banks and other functions are undamaged."

Cord opened his mouth to reply, but felt a faint touch of something soft on his hand. He looked down, and saw Samella reaching weakly up to him, grey eyes wide and staring.

"Couldn't...breathe..." she mumbled.

"It's all right now," Cord said gently. "Stay there till you're stronger."

The ghost of a crooked smile flitted over Samella's face. "Cord MaKiy," she murmured. "We made it."

"We did," Cord said firmly. "And so did GUIDE, or most of him. I'm going to look in the other caskets and see if there are any more...."

"Do not open the caskets," GUIDE broke in. "My readings show that there are four others still alive, aside from your two selves. But they are still in suspended animation. Normal life processes must be restored slowly, with care."

Cord felt chastened, realizing that he might have injured the others if he had blundered along opening caskets. But at the same time he felt a surge of delight. "Hear that?" he said happily to Samella. "There are more of us!"

She nodded slowly. She was breathing more easily, regaining her strength. But then she tried to raise herself, and grimaced.

"Can you help me?" she asked. "I feel like I've been pounded into powder."

Cord grinned and reached down, sweeping her up out of the casket with no apparent effort. As he set her on her feet, she raised her eyebrows. "Either I've lost weight, or you're stronger than you look."

Cord felt a little aggrieved. He was well aware of how he looked. In loose clothing, like the tunic he was wearing, the short stocky breadth of him made him look fat. Especially with the muscular thickness of his neck, and the slightly rounded youthfulness of his face.

But Samella had not noticed the effect of her words, for she had started moving slowly towards GUIDE.

"What happened, GUIDE?" she asked. "How did we survive?"

"The freighter's passage through atmosphere heated the hull to melting point," the computer replied, "and its space drive exploded."

Samella frowned. "Then why are we still here?"

"Eighteen seconds before the explosion," GUIDE continued, "the heat of the freighter's hull melted through the fastenings that held the shuttle. So the shuttle was released, and had fallen far enough away from the freighter to escape the explosion."

"Talk about random factors," Samella murmured. "Or just wild luck."

"When the shuttle was free," GUIDE added, "its own space-drive was activated. The retro-jets fired eleven seconds before it struck the vegetation. So the impact was reduced. The forward section—containing most of the supplies for your colony—suffered most of the damage."

"So much for our supplies," Samella said sourly.

"Maybe we won't need them," Cord suggested. "The planet might supply what we need. Let's have a look outside."

"Feeling caged in, wild man?" Samella asked,

with one of her crooked smiles. "All right, let's go look at our planet."

They crossed the area, towards what had been the airlock but was now a gaping hole with jagged metal edges. Shoulder to shoulder they stepped into the opening, and looked out at Klydor.

Cord's first impression was of ghostliness. Pale, dim, grey light, with grey-white swirls of mist. A deathly stillness, with the sense of vast stretches of silent emptiness on all sides.

His chest swelled as he took a deep breath. The air was laden with strange alien odours, but they were interesting rather than unpleasant. And the air was cool and moist, so that if Cord closed his eyes and ignored the smells, he might have been breathing the first damp air of an autumn morning in the Highlands. In fact it probably *was* morning, he thought, before the sunrise that might dispel the night mists.

He jumped down from the airlock opening, and Samella followed. The ground was soft and yielding turf, a little like long-stemmed moss, grey-green and springy.

And all around, as far as he could see, were the trees.

They had tall, straight trunks, smooth and greenish-brown. Some were slender saplings, some were thick and up to about thirty metres tall. Each seemed to have a bulge at the top of the trunk, like some whitish fungus in a bulbous, hemisphere shape. But Cord could not see the bulges clearly, for at the same spot the foliage of the trees sprouted.

Long narrow, tapering to a sharp point, the growths looked like leaves and branches both. They were shaped like oversized blades of grass—or like large sword-blades, Cord thought, for they shone silvery-white in the grey dawn. And they grew from the top of the trunk in a fringe, like a tall crown around that odd fungus-like bulge, each leaf-branch reaching up another two or three metres on the tallest trees.

It was a weird, alien landscape, but to Cord it was not disturbing. It was a forest, a wilderness. For the young Highlander, it was more like home than he could ever have dared to hope.

"We surely left our mark," Samella said.

He turned, following her gaze. The shuttle had crash-landed at the flat, skimming angle that had been programmed for it. And it had cut a long, open corridor through the forest—as if some giant scythe had swept through, leaving behind it a litter of fallen trees, torn, broken, crushed.

Finally the shuttle must have slewed sideways, crashing forward broadside for the last two hundred metres. When it came to rest, it had left behind it a broad clearing, carved by that last slashing sidewards slide.

They wandered out into the clearing, and Cord realized that he was enjoying himself. Though he kept a wary eye on the misty dimness of the forest, he was also taking pleasure in the soft turf, the cool air, most of all the prospect of exploring this wilderness and learning its secrets. Must be in the blood, he thought wryly—recalling all the tales of how the Highlanders had usually been the first trail-blazers, sent out by old Britain to carve colonies out of wildernesses.

On the edge of the clearing they paused, looking into the forest, where the leaf-branches allowed little of the morning light to filter through into the shadows. But there was light enough for Cord to see, with surprise, that there was no undergrowth, no other plants. Just the trees, and the turf.

"It looks almost...*tended*," he said. "Like a tree farm."

Samella did not reply. And when Cord turned to her, she was standing with her eyes squeezed shut, fingertips pressed to her temples.

"What is it?" Cord asked anxiously.

"A headache," she said, her voice tight. "It started when we left the shuttle." With an effort she controlled herself, opening her eyes. "It'll pass. What were you saying?"

"The forest," Cord said, still watching her worriedly. "It's so tidy. The trees all grow far enough apart to give their roots room. And there's no underbrush. And no *dead* trees."

Despite the pain that still showed in her eyes, Samella nodded. "You're right. But it *is* an alien forest." She glanced behind them, at the clearing. "And there are plenty of dead trees now."

"True enough," Cord said, feeling vaguely guilty at the havoc that the crash had caused. He stepped away, towards a fallen tree where the odd wrinkled fungus-growth was clearly visible among the smashed remains of the leaf-branches.

Behind him Samella moaned. He spun round to

see her half bent over, clutching her head, her face again twisted with pain.

"My head... getting worse," she said through clenched teeth. "A pressure, inside... like a scream...."

Cord took her arm, feeling cold with concern. Had she suffered some internal injury, maybe a skull fracture, in the crash? He knew he had only the crudest knowledge of first aid, and there was not likely to be anyone else on the shuttle with medical knowledge. And probably no medical supplies left intact in the wreckage.

"Come back to the shuttle," he said gently. "Rest a while. Maybe it's an after-effect of the crash."

Samella was holding the sides of her head as if afraid it would burst, but she nodded faintly. Half-supporting her, Cord turned back across the clearing towards the shuttle.

But as they drew near to the damaged craft, he halted, and shock flashed like electricity through his veins.

Standing in the airlock, staring out at them, were three of the strangest-looking creatures he had ever seen.

5

Responsibility

Three teenagers. And Cord's heart sank, because they looked like trouble.

The two boys were relaxed and slouching, but there was a cold watchfulness in their eyes. And the girl beside them seemed even more tense—standing with fists on hips, glaring. But it was their appearance as much as their stance that unsettled Cord.

Of the two boys, the shorter one had an odd ivory sheen to his skin, and the taller one was a coffee-coloured brown. Both seemed fit and wiry, lean muscle showing where they had left the ColSec tunics carelessly unfastened. Their heads were entirely hairless, and on each smooth dome was a ridged scar, like a worm beneath the skin, forming a letter—a J and an R. And, even more strangely, each boy had a small piece of silvery metal, shaped like an S, embedded in the skin of his forehead.

The face of the girl, who was short and sturdily

built, was at least as strange. Her hair looked like coarse black wire, cut short and bristling up from her scalp in all directions. And the skin of her face was streaked, or smeared, with what looked like thick black paint—a broad band across her forehead, another from cheek to cheek across the bridge of her nose, two vertical bands down her cheeks, two narrower bands on either side of her mouth. Yet the rest of her skin, on her hands and throat, was a pasty white, like mushrooms grown in darkness.

Cord watched them silently as he moved forward, and Samella moved slightly away from him, dropping her hands, as if the pain in her head had been forgotten with the arrival of the weird threesome.

"A fat fell' and a skinny chuck," the shorter youth said. His voice was sharp, with a hint of a sneer. "Not much to look at."

"Not much," the tall one echoed, in a rich baritone. "Seems they get on pretty good."

"Folk got to get on," the short one said, with a snort of mocking laughter.

Cord bristled, but tried to keep his voice calm. "I'm Cord MaKiy," he told them. "She's Samella Connel."

"Two names each," the tall boy said sourly. "Straight folk. That's *all* we need."

As Cord's jaw tightened, the angry-looking girl broke in. "Why don't you yecks ease off for a min?" she snarled, then turned back to Cord and Samella. "I'm Heleth—troop called the Vampires, from the Bunkers, old London." She waved a stubby hand at the wrecked shuttle. "What's been happening here?"

"We've crashed," Cord told her bluntly. "On a planet called Klydor..."

He was interrupted by a scornful laugh from the short boy. "You're jerkin' us, fats. Antarctica, that's where this is."

Anger flashed in Cord's eyes. "I'm telling you— it's another planet, where ColSec sent us. Use your eyes—did you ever see a forest like this on Earth?"

The tall boy looked around, frowning. "Jeko, it's s'posed to be all ice and snow, Antarctica..."

The shorter one, Jeko, snorted. "Maybe. So we crashed, gettin' there. They say there's lots of jungles and stuff south of the American Segment." He grinned jeeringly at Cord. "Me, I never saw a real tree in my life, fats. How should I know about forests?"

"There's a computer in the shuttle," Samella put in quietly. "Go ask it where we are."

Heleth had been staring wide-eyed at Cord since he had answered her question. Now she wheeled, with a muffled snarl, and stalked back into the shuttle. The two youths followed her, still with mocking grins, and Cord and Samella stepped up into the airlock and went after them.

They stood quietly, watching, while GUIDE's soft voice spoke, and the arrogance of the threesome began to crumple. Heleth still looked furious, but her hands had begun to shake, and she was gnawing her blackened lower lip as if to keep it from trembling. The tall boy turned pasty grey, and sagged, while Jeko looked like he was about to cry or scream or both, his face twisting with shock.

When GUIDE had finished, Jeko whirled to face Cord, madness in his eyes. "*You* decided!" he screeched. "*You* got us into this!"

He leaped forward in a manic rush, one fist slamming in a vicious karate punch at Cord's midriff. Cord could not have hoped to avoid it. But by reflex he tautened his stomach muscles against the impact. It was as if Jeko's fist struck solid teak. Cord staggered back a step, but nothing more.

And before Jeko had even registered that his furious punch had had no effect, Cord grasped him by his tunic, and the belt of his trousers and flung him with effortless ease, five metres across the floor, to crash painfully into his tall companion.

Both of them tumbled to the floor in a flurry of limbs and yells. But they were up again at once, in fighting crouches. And Jeko had snatched up one of the narrow shards of metal from the shattered forward wall of the shuttle, gripping it like a knife.

But before anyone could move, Heleth sprang forward, dark eyes flaming. "Put the blade down, you Limbo yeck!" she yelled. "You heard the computer! We're alive because this fell' saved us! *Saved* us! You want to chop him for *that?*"

The tall boy hesitated, then straightened slowly. "The chuck's right, Jeko," he said.

Jeko glanced at him, and some of the fighting madness went out of his eyes. "Maybe," he snarled. "But who needs it? Who wants to be alive, alone on a place like this?"

Samella glared at him scornfully. "Stop crying for yourself. Alive is always better than dead. And you're not alone here—unless you're going to use that blade on all of us. There're five of us, on a planet we know nothing about. We have to be together, not fight each other."

"Jeko . . ." the tall boy began.

"Yeah, I know, Rontal," Jeko said sourly. "This chuck's right, too." A flick of his wrist flung the metal shard away, clanging on to the floor, and Jeko looked Samella up and down. "Where you from, chuck? What's your troop?"

"No troop," Samella said. "I was an indent, in Minneap'. And the name's Samella. And this—" she glanced at Cord with a crooked smile—"is Cord, who's a barbarian from the Highlands."

Cord opened his mouth to protest, but Heleth interrupted, with a sudden, merry, gap-toothed grin. "Another Brit? There's a turn. Never saw one of you folk before."

"What's the Highlands?" asked Rontal, the tall youth.

"Far north from old London," Heleth told him. "A wild land full of wild folk. Even CeeDees don't go there." She turned her grin on Jeko. "You tangled with the wrong fell', Jeko."

Jeko studied Cord for a moment, then unexpectedly smiled. "Seems," he agreed. "And he's not so fat, neither."

Samella giggled at that—and then suddenly they were all laughing, even Cord, though he tried hard to remain stern. And as the laughter echoed around the metal-walled interior of the shuttle, it seemed that some of the fear and shock and tension that had existed in that area began to evaporate, to drift away like the mist among the alien trees outside.

Finally the laughter subsided, and the five young people looked at each other.

"Seems I got to say some sorries for what

happened," Jeko said at last. "Got a case of the means, wakin' up to all this." He waved a hand at the wreckage, and the smashed caskets, then looked at Cord. "That make it right between us?"

Cord blinked, a little confused by the slang, but nodded willingly.

"Right." Jeko beamed. "And I didn't even say who we are. But you know I'm Jeko, and this's Rontal." He reached up to touch the silvery S embedded in his forehead. "Free Streeters from Limbo. That's . . . ."

"We know," Samella broke in with a smile. "But not any more. Now you're like us—free citizens of the planet Klydor."

"There's a turn," Heleth said. "A little troop of our own, on a planet of our own."

"Not ours," Rontal growled. "ColSec's."

Heleth's statement had struck an echo, deep within Cord's being. But Rontal's remark left them all in sombre silence, until Jeko looked around, worriedly.

"So what do we *do*," he asked, "on this planet?"

Cord stared at him, and at the similarly concerned expressions on the faces of Heleth and Rontal. And then he understood. Though these kids were tough and smart and dangerous, they were *city* kids—from parts of Earth that were civilized, even though that civilization was shattered and crumbling. Here, on a wild planet, their urban knowledge and street-wise skills were just about useless. They were bewildered, and lost.

"What we do," Cord said bluntly, "is *survive*. And for that, to start with, we need three things—

food, water, shelter. We've got the third, here in the shuttle. Now we've got to go and explore, see if there's water in the forest that we can drink, and anything that we can eat."

"Sounds good," Jeko said, nodding.

But he and the other two were still looking at Cord, expectantly. And then Cord realized the further truth. They had spent most of their lives in gangs—troops, as they called them. And gangs had leaders. They were waiting for Cord to *lead* them.

No, he thought. Not me. In the Highlands there are no leaders, no followers. I wouldn't know how to lead if I wanted to. Or how to be led.

But Samella, at least, was not willing to give Cord the total power of decision-making. "I was thinking," she said quietly, "that we should look through there." She pointed to the crumpled hatchway leading to what was left of the shuttle's forward section. "Maybe some of our supplies survived the crash."

Cord agreed readily. But then he paused, a memory jolted by her words. "Samella, didn't GUIDE say there were *four* others who lived through the crash?"

Samella was shocked. "Of course... I completely forgot!"

They surveyed the jumble of caskets. Before, only two of the less damaged caskets had stood open—Cord's and Samella's. But now the lids on four others were raised. Three of them had held Jeko, Rontal and Heleth—but the last one was just as empty.

"Must have wakened up before us," Heleth said, "and went off somewhere."

"We didn't see anyone when we were out," Cord said with a frown. "Whoever it was must have gone into the forest when we were on the far side of the clearing."

"We'd better go out and look," Samella said.

Cord nodded, then remembered. "Some of us can go," he said. "What about your headache?"

"It's gone," she said, looking surprised as if she too had just remembered it. "It stopped when we got back into the shuttle."

"Could be something in the air out there," Cord said thoughtfully. "Maybe you should stay here while we make a search."

At first Samella demurred. But then Cord explained to the others, and they agreed that there would be no point in Samella risking more pain. So she agreed—partly because she had thought of something else.

"I suppose if I stay behind, I can find out a few things," she said. "GUIDE told us that he had all the details of the planet in his data banks. I can find out how much of that information survived the crash."

"That makes sense," Cord said. "Ask it about food and weather, things like that. And if there's anything dangerous in the forest."

Jeko grinned. "Fell', there's nothin' out there more dangerous'n a couple of Limbo Streeters."

"Except a Bunker Vampire," Heleth said sharply.

They all laughed again. And then Cord—careful to give no signal that might be seen as a leader's order—moved towards the airlock. The other three fell in behind him, as if they had been waiting for him to move.

They emerged into the clearing, and Cord was pleased to find that he had been right about the time of day. The mist had thinned to only a few wisps, and one edge of the sky was painted a luminous orange. There was a sun, and it was rising. But still, Cord noted, the forest was entirely silent—no birdsong or rustling of small creatures, maybe no life in there at all, except the trees.

So he was both watchful and a little excited as they moved across the clearing. And the others were also excited, fascinated by the alien landscape, but at the same time keeping up a stream of merry chatter that answered many of Cord's unasked questions. He learned that the Streeters were each sixteen, and that Heleth was a year older. He learned that Jeko descended from people called "nisei", who were Americans but somehow also a kind of Asians—and that Rontal would once have been called a "black". But that word seemed more suited to Heleth, whose facial darkening was not paint, Cord found, but something put under the skin. It was all interesting, though for Cord it all raised as many questions as it answered.

But then they reached the edge of the clearing, and the silent dimness of the forest put an end to their talk. Watchful, a little awed, the three of them peered in among the trees. And Cord saw that the other three were glancing at him, as if waiting to be told what to do.

He had no idea what to do about that. He

didn't want the responsibility, nor did he want any-one else to be responsible for him. He wanted the Highlands way, the free co-operation of equals, among people who most of the time went their own way. But how could he explain that to three kids from the close-knit city gangs of Earth?

He was still pondering the problem when the sound ripped through the silence around them.

Back in the shuttle, Samella had screamed.

6

The Leader

Cord reached the shuttle in a furious sprint, hurdling the fallen trunks of trees, so that the scream still seemed to be echoing within the interior as he leaped through the airlock, the others on his heels.

Samella was standing stiffly in front of the smashed screen of GUIDE. And she was facing a person who made Jeko and the others look almost ordinary.

A tall, broad-shouldered, bony man, with a shock of pure-white hair. Yet the face was youthful, despite its angular narrowness. It was also just about the ugliest face Cord had ever seen. Greyish-white skin, seeming more pallid because of a smear of lurid green tattooing on the hollow cheeks. Narrow, glittering eyes set deep in cavernous sockets. A wide mouth with thick, fleshy-red lips, and a flattened nose that seemed hardly a nose at all.

Cord saw all those details in one startled glance as he came to a halt. "Samella?"

"Sorry I screamed." Samella seemed nervous, but in control of herself. "He . . . he startled me."

"Scared you out of your pants, is what," the bony man said, grinning. The grin showed prominent, sharp canine teeth, almost like fangs.

"He's a Crusher," Rontal breathed from behind Cord.

Cord half-turned, puzzled, as the bony man smiled again.

"Smart kid," he said. "Recognized the tattoos."

Cord became aware that Samella had moved to stand next to him. "The Crushers are a special combat team, set up by the CeeDees—the Civil Defenders," she told him in a low voice. "If anyone sets up a group to resist the Organization, the Crushers are sent in. It happened a couple of years ago, in some oilfields west of where I lived." Her voice hardened. "They say the Crushers didn't leave a single person alive."

"Another smart kid," the bony man said, still grinning evilly. "I was there, in those oilfields. Somebody starts trouble, Crushers go in to stop it."

"By torture and killing," Samella said coldly.

The grin vanished. "Crushers are trained for killing, sweets," the man said, his voice sharp. "Best in the world. Don't you forget it." But as Samella met his gaze defiantly, the grin suddenly reappeared, as if a switch had been thrown. "But I'm not a Crusher now. Past year, I been battle chief of the Death Angels, the toughest, meanest troop in Quake City on the west coast. They call me the Lamprey, 'cause when I grab, the fell' stays grabbed."

Cord heard the hiss of breath through Jeko's

teeth as the man called the Lamprey identified himself. And the man turned his evil grin towards the sound.

"Figured you'd have heard of the Angels, kid." His glittering eyes swept over the faces of the two boys, and their scarred scalps. "Streeters from Limbo, right?" He giggled suddenly, an eerie sound that started and stopped abruptly. "Only troop that has to carve their initials on their heads, so they don't forget who they are."

Jeko nodded nervously. "Yeah. I'm Jeko, he's Rontal."

But the Lamprey's gaze had swung away, towards Heleth. "And you, shorty. What's the black face for?"

Heleth blinked, also looking nervous. "Heleth, from the Bunkers, old London. The black is a sub-skin injection, for camouflage in the tunnels."

The Lamprey giggled again, as if she had made a joke, and then looked at Cord. "How about you, chub? What's your troop?"

Cord glared. "Cord MaKiy, and I have no *troop*. I'm from north Britain, the Highlands."

The ugly grin twisted into a sneer. "Never heard of it." He looked at Samella. "You from these Highlands too, sweets?"

She shook her head coldly. "Minneap'. And no troop, either. I was an indent."

The Lamprey's high giggle rose. "What a bunch of dulls." Ignoring Cord's glower and Samella's tightened mouth, he glanced at the airlock. "So now we know who we are, time to find out *where*. When

I woke up I went out, for a look-see—and this place's got to be the back-end of the earth."

"It's not Earth," Cord said bluntly. "It's another planet, called Klydor."

Every muscle on the Lamprey's lean body went taut. The sneering smile narrowed into a grimace, and the glittering eyes were like hot coals in the sockets of a skull.

"*Planet?*" The word was a strangled yell.

"No one's had a chance to tell you," Samella said quickly. She turned to the computer console. "GUIDE, tell the . . . the Lamprey where we are."

As GUIDE's soft voice obligingly began, Cord watched the Lamprey's face, fascinated and repelled. Emotions seemed to flow over it, swift and changeable as water over rock. One moment he would be glaring, snarling, hands clenching into fists. The next second he would be showing his teeth in his evil grin, or bursting into one of his eerie giggles. And then the sudden rage again. . . .

As he watched, Cord realized with a nerve-twisting certainty that the Lamprey was insane.

The others realized it as well, he saw, and were glancing at one another nervously. But at the same time Cord could see that Heleth and the Streeters were impressed by the Lamprey, even in awe of him.

Then GUIDE finished the quiet recital, and the Lamprey swung away, shaking with fury. "They can't *do* that!" he raged. "They got no *right*! ColSec sends no-hope *kids* into space—not ex-Crushers! Not *me*!"

Cord was startled to realize that the existence of ColSec's callous methods was not news to the Lamprey—that his fury was simply at being included.

Then he was startled again when Samella spoke, her voice sharp with distaste.

"But you're here," she said. "With us no-hopers. Just another ColSec exile."

Cord braced himself, because the Lamprey's face was vicious and hate-filled, and Cord was sure that he would leap at Samella. But then, slowly, the bony body relaxed, and the thick lips stretched in another grin.

"Not for long, sweets," he said. "When ColSec gets here, they'll see they made a mistake, sending *me* with you dulls. Till then, we just make the best of it. Right?"

"Right," Jeko said eagerly. "That's what Cord said. We got to survive."

"Cord said we should explore the forest," Heleth added. "See what we can find to eat, and that."

"Cord said," the Lamprey repeated, in a tone that Cord did not care for. "You set up as the leader of this troop, MaKiy?"

Cord met his gaze steadily. "There is no leader. We don't need a leader."

"Wrong," the Lamprey snarled. "You need. And you got. The Lamprey's here."

"What if we don't want you?" Samella asked angrily. "Anyway, if we have to be *led*, it should be by someone who knows wild country, like Cord does. It's all forest, outside."

The Lamprey stared at her witheringly. "You wouldn't be stupid enough not to *want* the Lamprey, sweets. And I'll tell you why. First, I'm some over twenty, older'n any of you. Second, I was a Crusher, smarter and harder than all of you together. Third, I *was* a leader, with the Death Angels, where I reckon all of you were followers, in your troops, or nothing. Right?"

Jeko, Rontal and Heleth nodded dumbly.

"And fourth," the Lamprey went on, "there's nothing *but* wild country between Quake City and the American Segment. And I've crossed it more times than MaKiy, here, has sat down to supper. I reckon he could learn from me. So—what d'you say now, sweets?"

Samella glared, but said nothing.

"'Course," the Lamprey said, surveying the others with his evil grin, "there's a way for anyone to take over a troop, if they think they're good enough. They can fight the leader, head to head. So any of you want to take over, that's how you do it. Over top of me." He reached out with a long arm and prodded Cord's chest with a sharp-nailed forefinger. "How about you, chub?"

No one moved, or breathed, and the tension in the air seemed almost solid. But Cord stared back at the glittering eyes, trying to sound calm.

"We went through all that before you turned up," he said. "There's no point fighting among ourselves. We have to get along, to survive."

The Lamprey giggled. "That means you don't want to fight, right?"

Cord did not reply. He had seen Samella look at him anxiously, when the Lamprey had first challenged him. But now she turned her gaze away, and there seemed to be a shadow across her eyes.

She thinks I'm afraid, Cord thought unhappily. And maybe I am. But I don't see the point of getting killed trying to stop this maniac from being leader. Especially when I don't want to be leader myself.

But as those thoughts were swirling through his mind, the Lamprey was beginning his leadership.

"If that's all settled," he said, grinning around at them all, "time to get doing things. What about supplies and stuff?"

"Our supplies were in there," Samella said coldly, pointing to the crushed front of the shuttle.

The Lamprey nodded. "Some of us can go see if anything's left that we can use. Sweets, you were messing with the computer when I came back. You know about that stuff?"

When Samella nodded wordlessly, the Lamprey's fanged grin widened. "So you're some use after all, even if you got a smart mouth. Too bad you're not pretty." Samella's eyes blazed as the Lamprey giggled. "You can find out what the computer knows about this planet, and I'll take these two—" pointing at Jeko and Heleth—"to see what we can dig out of the mess up front."

"And me?" Cord asked evenly.

"You, chub, get the garbage detail." The Lamprey gestured with a long hand at the heap of crushed caskets. "You and this Limbo baldy here—" a sneering glance at Rontal—"can go out and dig a nice deep hole. Then you can dump all these blank-heads who got killed in the crash, and cover them up. Caskets and all."

Cord looked at him emptily for a moment, then shrugged and turned away, followed by Rontal—and by another of the short, eerie giggles.

*   *   *

The work came as a relief to Cord. He and Rontal were digging—out in the clearing, some distance from the airlock of the shuttle—with makeshift spades that were two larger shards of broken metal. And the steady, sweaty effort of using his muscles helped to calm his tension. He tried not to think, merely to dig, in silence. And Rontal, too, had withdrawn into himself, so they did not exchange a word during all the hours it took to carve deep into the reddish soil beneath the turf.

As those hours went by, under the hot orange sun of Klydor, hunger and raging thirst began to affect both diggers. Until Heleth appeared at the edge of the deepening pit, with strange containers in her hands. They held clear water and a porridgy kind of food, and Heleth cheerfully told Cord and Rontal the news as they ate and drank.

Some of their supplies had, after all, survived the crash. There were packs of food concentrate, crushed but unharmed, and containers of water that had been stored frozen. There was even a medi-kit, almost intact, and a few specialized electronic tools—which Samella was now using in her work on GUIDE.

"Has she learned anything yet?" Cord asked.

"Not much," Heleth said. "Just that this's an Earth-type planet, most ways." She glanced over her shoulder. "I got to get back. The Lamprey told me not to hang around out here."

"Could be Earth-type food and water on this planet, then," Cord said to Rontal as Heleth hurried away.

"And maybe Earth-type other things," Rontal replied gloomily. "Like animals. Monsters."

Cord's voice hardened. "Seems to me we've brought our own monster with us."

By what turned out to be mid-afternoon—for the days seemed more or less the same length as on Earth—the pit was deep enough. Then Cord and Rontal faced the gruesome task of carrying out the crushed caskets, with their mangled human contents. When they picked up the first one, Rontal staggered a little under its weight, and his dark eyes flickered when he saw that Cord had hoisted up his end with no apparent effort. But the tall Streeter made no comment—not until more time had passed, and all the caskets with the dead youths in them had been deposited in the pit, and the soft earth laboriously heaped over them.

Only then, in the gathering shadows of the late afternoon, with the mist stealing back among the trees beyond the clearing, did Rontal pause and look darkly at Cord.

"You're a strong fell'," he said. When Cord shrugged and said nothing, Rontal went on. "But you got smarts, too. What you did this morning was smart. 'Cause strong's not enough, against a Crusher. Fell' like that, he's trained every way there is, to kill. Most of all close up, with hands."

Cord looked at him bleakly. "Is that supposed to make me feel better?"

Rontal shook his head. "Nobody feels good about backin' off. Nobody feels good about bein' dead, neither. You made your choice. That's all you had."

He turned and strode away towards the shuttle.

And Cord felt a little ashamed of his surly response. So he broke into a jog, to catch up with Rontal, trying to find the right words to say. But they were never spoken.

Rontal had stopped, staring tensely at the airlock. And Cord stopped as well, tension gripping him just as hard.

The Lamprey was standing in the opening, holding a strange object in his hand. It was like a short bulky cylinder of plastic and metal, with odd protrusions coming out of it, including a long slim tube jutting from one end.

"Look what I found, chub," the Lamprey said, his evil smile flashing.

"What is it?" Cord asked Rontal quietly.

"Laserifle," Rontal grunted.

"Works, too," the Lamprey said. In a blur of motion he raised the weapon—and from the slender tube a beam of lethal, focused light leaped out, directly at Cord.

7

Forest-dwellers

Cord slept very little during that first night on Klydor. He felt he would never erase the memory of the laser beam's vicious hiss, as it sliced through the air only centimetres past his ear. Nor would he forget the grinning mockery of the Lamprey.

"Don't know if you're yellow or smart, chub!" the white-haired creature had yelled, with another manic giggle. "If you'd tried to duck, you might've moved right into the beam!"

Cord had thought of that as well, in a cold wave of delayed shock. Even so, he merely stood there, silent, gritting his teeth. And at last the Lamprey had grown tired of tormenting him, and they had all gone in, to spend a miserable evening in the shuttle.

The atmosphere had been alive with tension all evening, made worse by the Lamprey's constant cruel jibes. Clearly the maniac was trying to provoke someone—preferably Cord, but not necessarily. It was as if he needed violence, like a drug, Cord thought. Now he's got that rifle, he won't be happy unless he can *use* it. And we're his only available living targets.

The others had remained mostly silent, like Cord, sitting apart from one another. Even Samella had lost her earlier defiance, and seemed tired and withdrawn, not looking in Cord's direction. Nor were any of the others. So a feeling of isolation was added to Cord's burden of anger, humiliation and anxiety.

He even began to think that it might be better if he simply went off on his own. His absence might ease some of the tension. Also, it was the Highland way—to walk alone, to avoid the restrictions and leaders of group living. And he was confident that he could survive somehow, even in an alien wilderness.

But he was not sure that he could just walk away from the others, especially Samella, and leave them to the mercy of the Lamprey. So as he sat there, alone and silent, he was torn with indecision and misery—until the Lamprey interrupted his thoughts.

By then the others were removing the padding from the caskets that they had travelled in, to make crude beds on the metal floor. The Lamprey grinningly ordered Samella to prepare his bed in the same way, and she had begun to obey, without a word or a change of expression. Then the Lamprey ordered Cord to clear a space for the bed, amid the rubble and wreckage of the forward section.

"Wouldn't want anyone to get tempted, tonight, by my property here," the Lamprey said with a giggle, patting the laserifle.

Cord had quelled his sudden surge of anger, and had done as he was told. And when he had squeezed through the crumpled hatchway, into the forward area, what he found almost made him forget his problems.

The entire front half of the shuttle had been crushed inwards, pushed back so that instead of being an area about twenty metres across, it was now only about five metres. Most of the hull had been split open, and the smashed containers that had held their supplies were covered with broken metal and fragments from the shattered interior walls.

It's a miracle anything survived in here, Cord thought. Then he remembered the laserifle, and knew that it was one part of the miracle he could have done without.

Unhappily, angrily, he set to work obeying the Lamprey's order. He had nearly finished clearing a narrow space when Samella came through the hatchway, dragging the loose padding for the Lamprey's bed. Setting it down, she went wordlessly out again, returning in a moment with what looked like an armful of metallic junk.

"What's all that?" Cord asked, trying to sound casual.

"Spare bits from damaged laserifles he found," she replied briefly, "for replacement parts. And two spare power packs for the rifle. Now he can keep that weapon going for years."

Her voice had been flat, and she had still not

looked in Cord's direction. Without another word, she turned and went out.

Cord felt sick, and somehow betrayed by her coldness and withdrawal. *If this is what life will be on Klydor,* he thought wretchedly, *I'd as soon be out there in the pit with the ones who didn't make it.*

But somehow he got through that first tense and miserable night. And in the morning the Lamprey raised everyone's spirits a little by announcing that they would spend their second day exploring the forest. Since Cord had been aching to do just that since he had first stepped out of the shuttle, he was feeling almost eager when they finally set out.

The Lamprey led the way, laserifle held jauntily over one shoulder, as they crossed the clearing with its clutter of crushed and broken trees. Halfway across, Heleth noticed that Samella's lips were pressed tight, and that there were lines of pain around her eyes.

"What's the trouble?" the dark girl asked.

"Headache," Samella said through clenched teeth. "Like I had before, when I left the shuttle."

The others turned to look. "Maybe you should go back..." Heleth began.

"She stays!" the Lamprey snapped. "I like my troop to keep together, so I know what everyone's doing."

He turned away, and the others followed. Samella was clearly still in pain, but fighting to control herself, as if determined not to show weakness in front of the Lamprey. Admiration for her toughness again grew within Cord—along with a new flood of helpless rage and misery.

They moved past the edge of the ragged clearing, into the forest, where the morning mist was thinning as sunlight filtered into the dimness. The springy turf, and the absence of other plants in the spaces among the trees, made walking easy. In other circumstances, Cord knew, he would be enjoying himself. He also felt hopeful when, farther into the forest depths, they found a small rivulet of clear water. But no one was willing to risk tasting it—and no one had seen anything that looked like food. Just the trees, and the turf.

But here and there Cord saw that the ground bulged upwards into long, rounded humps, as if there were things shaped vaguely like cylinders buried just under the soft turf. They were all of different sizes— some no larger than Cord's forearm, others much bigger and bulkier. And Cord realized that they looked like logs, with the turf grown over them. So there *are* dead trees, he thought, and felt a little better about the eerie strangeness of the forest.

And he felt better still when, a kilometre farther into the forest, they saw their first Klydor life form—a cloud of flying things about the size of moths, bluish-coloured and heavy-bodied. They settled peacefully on the trunk of a tall tree, and the group inspected them with interest, pleased to find that the silent, shadowy trees harboured some kind of living thing besides themselves.

Then, almost at once, they spotted another creature—a brown-furred, wide-bodied animal about the size of a rabbit but with twice as many legs. It

moved in a slow, comic waddle, until it reached the
tree where the fat blue flying things were resting.
Then it went up the tree-trunk like a frightened cat.
Clinging to the trunk with sharp little claws, it
chewed busily at the flying creature it had caught,
with a foolish expression on its snub-nosed face that
made Samella laugh despite her headache, and even
brought a smile to Cord's lips.

Until the Lamprey raised the laserifle and shot
it.

Samella wheeled on him, furious. "You didn't
have to do that!"

"I do what I want, sweets," the Lamprey said,
with an ugly grin. "And *you* do what I want. Remember that." He gestured with the rifle. "Jeko, go
pick it up."

As Jeko moved away, Samella looked directly at
Cord for the first time since the previous afternoon.
There was anger in her eyes, and an edge of pain,
and something else that Cord could not fathom. But
before he could find anything to say, Jeko yelped.

The small furry thing had fallen near one of the
turf-covered mounds that Cord had thought were
buried logs—one of the smaller ones, less than a
metre long. The furry thing had not been killed
outright, and was lying on the turf, jerking and
kicking in agony. But that was not what had startled
Jeko. It was because the buried log had *moved*.

The front end of it reared up, out of the turf. It
was a living cylinder, thick and flexible like an
oversized worm. Cord saw that it was segmented,
and covered with a kind of thick shell, dark brown
and shiny, which was also segmented, like separate

plates of what seemed to be a solid natural armour. It was eyeless, with a spray of thin tendrils, like antennae, sprouting from the front of its head. And on the underside of the head was a wide, gaping mouth, surrounded by longer, sturdier tendrils, more like tentacles. Each tentacle had a sharp, barbed hook at the end of it.

Still half-reared, the creature slid swiftly forward. Cord saw the small hooks on its underside, which pulled it along in an oozing slither, disturbingly silent. Ignoring Jeko, the worm-thing headed for the twitching form of the furry beast. One of the tentacles around the repulsive mouth struck out like a snake, the barbed hook driving into the furry body. The little creature convulsed, a final spasm that almost lifted it from the ground, then sank back into stillness. And the worm-thing lowered its gaping mouth on to the body.

"Yeck," Heleth said with feeling.

"Reckon those hook-things're poisonous," Rontal growled.

"Who cares?" the Lamprey snapped. "Out of the way, Jeko." He raised the rifle and took aim.

The beam struck dead centre on the worm-thing's turf-covered back. But nothing happened. Only the turf was scorched and burnt—and through it Cord glimpsed more of the shiny-brown shell.

"That thing's tough as space-steel," the Lamprey snarled. He strode forward, and his foot lashed out in a blurring kick at the feeding worm-thing. At once the creature reared up again, two of the hooked tentacles lashing out. But though it had struck so swiftly that Cord could hardly follow the movement, the Lamprey was even quicker. Leaping away from the deadly barbs, he fired from the hip into the centre of the mouth.

The worm fell away, rolling. Then it reared up again, tendrils slashing at the air, but its movements were slower, more erratic. And when the Lamprey fired once more, into that gaping mouth, it fell away and lay still, the tentacles limp.

"Are you going to kill off all the life forms on this planet?" Samella asked coldly.

The Lamprey grinned mockingly. "Might be a nicer place to live if I did."

"You'd be busy, Lamprey," Heleth said uneasily. "There's hundreds of those things."

They all looked around. Among the trees where they were standing, they could see about three dozen of the cylindrical, turf-covered mounds. Must be more like thousands of them, altogether, in the forest, Cord thought. And if they aren't fallen logs, the further thought came, then what *does* happen to dead trees?

But then he turned to watch as the Lamprey went over to kick brutally at another smaller mound. The kick jolted it, but it did not rear up to expose its menacing mouth. It remained unmoving.

The Lamprey giggled. "Asleep, or dead, or maybe not hungry. Anyway, these things aren't big enough to worry us."

"I wonder if there's anything out here," Rontal said edgily, "that *is?*"

The question seemed to remain in the air around them as they pushed deeper into the forest. But some while passed, and they saw no other creatures except more of the small turf-covered worm-things—all of them motionless, rock-like, impossible to disturb by a prod or a kick.

But then they came to a place where they learned that not all worm-things were small.

At first Cord thought it was simply a rise in the land. A smoothly rounded hillock of turf, the top of it higher than Rontal's scarred head, and more than twice as broad as it was high. But then Cord looked again and caught his breath, recognizing the shape.

The Lamprey saw the look on his face and followed his gaze. "Now look at that," he said, with a grin. "The big daddy of all the crawlies in the forest."

Again the laserifle flashed up, and the beam struck out. Turf blazed up briefly on the side of the immense hillock. And when it subsided, the glint of shiny-brown shell was obvious.

"It is!" Heleth breathed. "Lamprey, don't wake it up!"

But the titanic mound showed no signs of moving. And as the others relaxed, Jeko sidled forward— and suddenly leaped, scrambling up the side of the huge hump of turf. On the rounded top, he glanced round at the others, then stamped his foot.

"C'mon, monster!" he shouted. "Wake up! Take me for a ride!"

"Have you for dinner, more like," Heleth told him, as the others began to laugh.

But then Jeko saw that the Lamprey was glowering impatiently, and he slid quickly down. "So long, big fell'," he said to the motionless mound. "Sleep a *long* time."

The group moved away, Cord trailing in the rear. He was staring even more watchfully around at the forest, wondering what new strangeness, or menace, might next emerge from the shadows. And they had travelled less than half a kilometre farther when he had his answer.

He barely caught the distant movement, at the edge of his vision, but it was enough. He wheeled— and froze. And the others also went rigid, as they followed his gaze. Only Samella spoke aloud.

"Aliens!"

There were about a dozen of them, silent and watchful in the forest shadows about a hundred metres away. They were squat and solid-bodied, stooping slightly, with small heads jutting forward from powerful shoulders. Their arms and legs were long and sinewy, and their large, gnarled hands and feet had too many fingers and toes. Their skins were a pasty grey-blue, like mould, though most of their bodies were covered in a thick pelt of woolly hair, a dark blue-black. And their faces were frightening— huge round staring eyes like dark mirrors, no noses, wide mouths that drooped open to reveal curved and sharp-pointed teeth.

But they were empty-handed, and did not seem threatening. The two groups simply stared at one another, while Cord struggled with the numbing chill that came with the realization that the forest of Klydor was inhabited.

Then the Lamprey broke the frozen silence. "I've

seen ugly," he snarled, "but these blank-heads are it."

And before anyone could speak or move, he swung the laserifle up and fired its deadly beam into the alien group.

8

Alien Attack

Three of the beings crumpled silently. Others fell back, clutching wounds, with cries like the squalling of angry cats. But a few, protected by tree trunks from the sweeping beam, melted silently away into the shadows.

But before then, while the alien cries were still echoing through the forest, mingling with Samella's shriek of outrage, Cord had lunged forward. Hardly knowing what he was doing, he wrenched the rifle out of the Lamprey's hands, and swung a crashing backhand blow against the side of the man's narrow jaw.

Taken totally by surprise, the Lamprey was hurled backwards, slamming against the bole of a sturdy tree. For a moment his eyes glazed, and his knees buckled.

Behind him there was a murmur, as if of approval. But Cord did not turn to see who had made it. The Lamprey was recovering. A trickle of blood ran from the thick-lipped mouth, and the deep-set eyes were flaring with homicidal fury.

"I'm going to shred you, MaKiy," the Lamprey hissed, "and feed you to the worms."

He dropped into a crouch, one side of his face twitching madly. And Cord might have used the rifle, then, without a second thought—except that he had no idea how to fire one. Instead, he hefted it like a club, while knowing it would be little use against the deadly combat skills of the ex-Crusher.

But before either of them could move, Heleth's voice stopped them.

"Look! The aliens!"

The urgency in her voice sliced through even the Lamprey's manic fury. The glittering eyes shifted, and widened, and Cord too turned to look.

The forest seemed suddenly full of the stooping, humanoid shapes. About forty of them, Cord guessed—and with a difference. These aliens had objects like blades in their gnarled hands. And Cord realized that the objects were segments of the sharp-pointed leaf-branches of the trees. They had been trimmed so that the stout stems jutted a little, like hilts, making the weapons look like short swords.

Warily, but steadily, the forest beings were filtering among the trees, towards the humans.

"Give me that rifle, MaKiy!" the Lamprey snarled.

"No chance!" Cord snapped. "Samella—can you use this thing?" And when the girl nodded, wide-eyed, he tossed the laserifle to her. "Then use it. But just scare them off, keep them back, so we can get to the shuttle."

"You want to *run?*" the Lamprey sneered. "From a bunch of big-eyed uglies?"

Cord glared at him. "You think you can kill them all? We don't know how many more there are—and they know this forest better than we do."

"Makes sense," Jeko muttered. He and Rontal loped swiftly away, with Heleth following. For a moment, again, the madness returned to the Lamprey's eyes as he faced Cord. But Samella had stepped back out of reach, and now she raised the rifle and aimed it between the Lamprey's glittering eyes.

"Do what he says, Lamprey," she ordered. "Back to the shuttle."

For a second Cord thought that the madman might even spring directly at the muzzle of the rifle. But perhaps it was the cold anger in Samella's steady gaze that held him back.

And then there was no more time. The forest silence was torn apart by a chorus of savage, howling shrieks, as the aliens abandoned their wary advance and charged.

Instantly, coolly, Samella swung the rifle and fired—into the ground, in front of the leaders of the charge. The turf erupted into sudden, short-lived flame. And the leaders halted, falling back with howls of terror, and vanished with the others behind the shelter of tree-trunks. In that lull, the humans turned and fled.

Heleth and the Streeters were now out of sight, and the Lamprey sprinted after them at an astonishing speed. But Cord doubted that it was from fear. More likely, he thought, he wants to get back to the shuttle and set up some surprise for me. But he pushed that thought away, and glanced back.

The aliens were not pursuing. In fact they did not even seem to be looking at the retreating humans. They were staring upwards, looking oddly as if they were listening to something that Cord could not hear. Then they turned and filtered away through the shadows, almost at once lost to view.

Cord and Samella slowed their pace to a swift walk. Samella was as silent as ever, not looking at Cord, and he felt his gloom and misery returning as before. But he was more concerned with keeping a careful watch on the forest around them, in case the aliens were circling around, intending to ambush them. So he jumped, startled, when Samella spoke.

"The Lamprey will try to kill you now, for certain," she said.

Cord glanced at her. Taut lines of pain on her face showed that the strange headache had not left her, but she seemed to be controlling it. And Cord strove to keep his own voice just as calm.

"Maybe," he said. "But only if I go back."

Samella turned, frowning. "What do you mean?"

"It might be best if I left," Cord said flatly. "Aliens or no."

"You'd just walk away?" Samella asked, staring.

Cord shrugged. "Why not? Like you said, the Lamprey won't let me get away with what I did. And I don't feel like getting killed—whatever kind of coward I seem, to you and the others."

Samella was silent for a moment. "Is that what you think I feel?" she said at last.

"That's how you've acted," Cord said bluntly.

"Like you couldn't speak to me or even look at me, because I shamed myself by backing down."

Samella's lips tightened. "You ignorant . . . *barbarian!*" she said hotly. "I don't know or care about the others, but the *last* thing I wanted was for you to fight that killer. When he challenged you, I was terrified that you *wouldn't* back off. And then I kept quiet, and kept away from you, so he wouldn't think we were conspiring against him."

Cord's eyes had grown wide during this outburst. "So . . . you don't think I'm a coward?" he asked at last, lamely.

"Even if I had," Samella replied, "I wouldn't now, after what just happened."

Cord had begun to grin a huge relieved grin, but that reminder brought him back to reality. "But now, because of that, I *do* have to leave. Or fight."

"You can't leave," Samella told him fiercely. "We need you. You're used to forests and wild places. And you can make decisions—GUIDE proved that, by waking *you*, in space. We need you to help us deal with the Lamprey."

"You keep saying 'we'," Cord said. "But the others don't seem bothered."

"They're just keeping their heads down, hoping for the best," Samella assured him. "You really don't know much about people, do you? They're terrified of the Lamprey, too, because he's dangerously insane, and because not one of them would last a minute against him, hand to hand. So if you fought him, they'd stay neutral, in case he won."

"In case?" Cord laughed bitterly. "Of course

he'd win. *Will* win—because if I stay, I'll have to fight him."

"No, you won't." Samella's voice was firm. "Because I have the rifle now."

Cord looked at her wonderingly, and then a thought struck him. "He can't make another rifle, can he? From those spare parts you showed me?"

She shook her head. "They're just replacement parts, and spare power packs—not enough to build a whole rifle." She grinned fiercely, hefting the weapon in her hand. "This is the only laserifle on Klydor, as far as I know, and I mean to hold on to it."

"Would you use it on him?" Cord asked.

"If I had to."

Cord saw the grim, steady look in her eyes, and knew that she spoke the simple truth. And he smiled, but there was respect and admiration in his voice. "Seems that if anyone should be leader of this group, it's you."

"That's true," Samella said, with one of her crooked smiles. "Except I don't believe in leaders, and I don't think you do either. I think we believe in things like sharing, and co-operation, and partnership. But the other three come from the city gangs, where there are always leaders. And I think they'll follow you more easily than me."

"Maybe they can learn differently, in time," Cord said. "Like I'm learning—so much that I sometimes feel I can't take it all in."

"We're all learning," Samella said gravely. "It's the only way to live. We've got all Klydor to learn about—if the aliens let us. And if we can do something about the Lamprey."

"Well," Cord said, taking a deep breath, "let's go and get started."

But their start was delayed. As they drew near to the clearing they saw Jeko, moving uneasily among the trees, staring around. When he spotted them, he jogged forward, looking relieved.

"Where you been?" he said. "Thought the aliens got you."

"They stopped chasing us," Cord said, "so we took our time."

Jeko seemed hardly to have heard him. "We got a problem. Clearing's full of aliens. We're cut off from the shuttle."

Appalled, Cord set off at a swift lope, the others keeping pace. And soon he saw the problem for himself.

The clearing held more than a hundred of the huge-eyed forest beings, all of them hard at work— clearing away the trees crushed and felled by the shuttle's crash. Two or three at a time, they were picking up the shattered trunks—almost tenderly— and carrying them into the forest. And Cord saw more aliens working at the same task, along the broad corridor cut through the forest by the shuttle's slide.

By then the clearing was almost bare, except for some ragged stumps, splintered leaf-branches and other minor litter. And Cord noticed that the aliens were not concerned about the lower portions of any trees that had been broken in two. Only the upper segments, that held the strange fungus-growths, drew their almost gentle attention.

"Where are they taking them?" Samella whispered.

"We didn't follow any, to find out," Jeko said sarcastically. "They're not the problem."

Cord saw what he meant. About forty other aliens were not at work among the fallen trees. They were gathered near the open airlock of the shuttle, peering warily in, growling among themselves. And that group—probably the ones who had attacked them in the forest, Cord thought—was carrying the sword-like weapons made from the leaf-branches.

"They know we're out here," Jeko muttered. "They're prob'ly waiting for us to try for the shuttle."

By then Rontal and Heleth had joined them, and Cord glanced around. "Where's the Lamprey?"

"Right here," said a snarling voice behind him.

Cord wheeled. The Lamprey had materialized, silently, out of the shadowed trees. His glittering eyes fixed on Samella, whose grip had tightened on the rifle.

"You're going to have to use that gun, girl," he said.

Samella shook her head firmly. "They might never have attacked us if you hadn't shot at them. And we can't kill them all off. We'll just wait. Maybe when they've finished clearing away the trees, they'll go away and leave us alone."

The Lamprey sneered. But before he could speak, they heard another eruption of bestial howling from a group of aliens on the far side of the clearing. And when they turned, they saw that three of the thick, turf-covered worm-things were moving into the clearing, oozing along in their ghastly silent slither, heading for a cluster of fallen trees.

The armed group of aliens left the shuttle, and darted towards them, howling and screeching. At once the worms reared up, deadly hooked tentacles flailing. But the aliens did not hesitate. They sprang at the creatures, the leaf-blades stabbing at the gaping mouths, and at the joints between the segmented armour-plating of the shell. Several of the aliens fell back at once, as the lethal barbed hooks sank into their flesh, and lay writhing and convulsing on the ground. But the others did not pause, in their frantic and furious battle.

Within moments two of the worm-things, both small ones, lay motionless, a watery slime seeping from their wounds. But the third one was bigger— two metres long, and as thick as Cord's thigh—and its whipping tentacles were keeping the aliens at bay. By then nearly ten aliens were writhing on the ground, but their weapons had been snatched up by ten others, who had instantly, fearlessly, joined the battle. Yet they were losing. They could not get close enough, past the flashing sweeps of those venomous tentacles, to stab at the larger worm's vulnerable areas. And slowly, steadily, the worm was continuing to move, as it fought—heading for a tree that was bent but not broken, leaning at a steep angle on the clearing's edge.

Screeching even louder in their frenzy, the aliens battled on, more and more of them falling as the tentacles' barbs found their mark, but always being replaced. Then finally it was too late. The worm slithered up the angled trunk, climbing swiftly with the aid of the sharp hooks on its underside. And Cord stared with sickened fascination as it reached the top, and settled its repulsive mouth on to the fungus growth that crowned the trunk.

"Now's our chance!" the Lamprey said. While the others had been watching the chilling battle, he had seen that the shuttle had been left unguarded. Heleth and the Streeters followed as he sprinted away across the clearing.

But Cord did not join them. Samella was slumped against a tree, face twisted with pain and pale as death. The rifle dangled loosely from her hand, and Cord was grateful that the Lamprey had been too concerned about the shuttle to notice. He stepped quickly towards her, knowing that the pain did not affect Samella when she was inside the shuttle. So he flung a muscular arm around her waist and, half-lifting her from her feet, set off in an awkward jog across the clearing.

He was less than halfway across when he heard the alien cries change their tone. Glancing back, he felt icy fear sweep over him.

Snarling and screeching, brandishing their leaf-blade weapons, some three dozen of the alien beings were charging across the open space towards him.

9

Night Watch

Even through her pain, Samella seemed aware of the danger, and tried to speed her staggering pace, still being half-carried by Cord. But the laserifle, drooping from her hand, became tangled with her feet, and she tripped, dragging Cord off balance. He stumbled, and had to release her so they would not both sprawl on the turf.

And in that moment, they saw that they would not make it.

As the screeching aliens bore down upon them, Cord stooped swiftly. On the ground before him lay a sturdy length of torn-up root from one of the felled trees. Its butt end was as heavy as the head of a club, and the haft was as thick as his own wrist. He snatched it up, and sprang to meet the rush of the aliens.

Many people would have needed two hands to wield that weapon, but Cord swung it one-handed as if it were a slender switch. The club whistled as he flailed it in front of him, back and forth in a sweeping arc.

The charging aliens were halted by that furious barrier. And Cord drove them back, maintaining the slashing sweeps of the club. Two of them tried to circle and attack him from the side, but he leaped at them, the club thumping into the wide flat chest of one of them, hurling the creature off its feet to collide heavily with the other. By then Cord had sprung back to face the main body of attackers, again keeping them at bay with the menacing club.

But then the aliens divided into separate groups, to come at him from opposite sides. With a yell of rage, Cord leaped at one group—but they held their ground, striking with their leaf-weapons at the flailing club. And there were enough of them to jolt Cord's arm, to slow the club's furious pendulum swing.

In that instant, the second group of aliens hurled themselves at Cord's unprotected back.

But they did not reach him.

Cord heard a wild yell like a battle-cry, and three figures like vengeful furies flashed past him. Jeko, Rontal and Heleth had come to join the battle.

Each of them had sharp metal fragments, from the shuttle's wreckage, glinting like knives in their hands. And their arrival halted the second group of aliens in their tracks, in a moment of sudden surprise and confusion.

In that moment, Cord backed towards the other three, so that they were standing as if on the four corners of a square, weapons poised and waiting.

"'Bout nine to one odds, I make it," Jeko said conversationally.

"Like that time in the alley, last year," Rontal replied, just as casually.

But then the momentary pause came to an end. The aliens, growling fiercely, had again regrouped, and were crouching, gripping their own blades in a menacing wall of sharp deadliness. And Cord planted his feet, awaiting the charge that would probably overwhelm them.

But it did not come. He heard instead the humming hiss of the laser beam as it flashed past him, once again causing flame to explode up from the turf at the aliens' feet. They stumbled back, as before, their howls rising into shrillness. And again and again the beam lanced out—slicing a leaf-blade in two, searing across a thick hairy shoulder, stabbing again with fiery effect into the turf.

As the smoke and flame rose, they were finally too much for the alien attackers. Screeching, they broke and fled, pursued across the clearing by bursts of flame as the laser beam fired into the turf behind them.

Jeko was laughing delightedly as the four of them turned to Samella. She was half-sitting, half-lying on the turf, her face still contorted with pain—but her jaw was set tightly, and the rifle was steady in her hands as she fired a final blast towards the trees where the alien attackers had disappeared.

"You just went and spoiled all the fun," Rontal said in a mock-grumble.

But Samella ignored him. The lean figure of the Lamprey had emerged from the shuttle, moving towards them. And Samella's fierce, pain-filled expression did not change as she swung the rifle around, aiming it unwaveringly at the white-haired man.

"Keep your distance, Lamprey," she said through gritted teeth. "You're not boss here any more."

The Lamprey's giggle was mirthless, chilling. "Who is? You, sweets? Or chub, there?"

"No one," Cord said firmly, stepping over next to Samella. "We're all in this together, and that's the way it should be." He glanced at the other three, who had again grown silent and watchful. "You came out to help me because you wanted to, not because some *leader* ordered you to. Right?"

They looked at him blankly, then nodded. "Just seemed the thing to do," Heleth said.

"It was," Cord replied. "And I thank you. Because that's what we have to think about—what is the thing to do. We have a lot of problems in this place—all the more now, with the aliens, thanks to the killer here." He flung a cold look at the Lamprey. "If we're going to survive, and have any kind of life here, we have to work *together*. Because we want to. Not because some crazy with a gun is telling us to."

The Lamprey's eyes flared hotly at the word "crazy". But he grinned one of his vicious, sharp-toothed grins. "Big words, MaKiy. But I'm listening only 'cause sweets there has the rifle. And you'd better listen to this. You and sweets can't watch me *all* the time. Soon enough, you'll slip up. And when you do—"the fanged grin widened—"you'll wish you'd let the aliens finish you."

*   *   *

Some hours later, darkness had fallen over the forest of Klydor, and the night mist drifted in streamers over the empty clearing. Inside the shuttle, the group had made a silent and edgy meal from the food concentrate, and soon afterwards the day's tensions had taken their toll. Rontal, Jeko and Heleth were sprawled on their makeshift beds, deeply asleep.

But Cord sat silently next to the open airlock, the laserifle across his lap. He was as weary as the others, but there would be no sleep for him for a while. Samella had shown him how to fire the rifle, and he was now standing guard—against two separate dangers.

For one, the aliens were still roaming and prowling, among the trees just beyond the clearing. They had been spotted by Heleth, whose underground life had given her an ability to see in the dark that seemed almost magical. And while Cord did not think that the forest beings would attack the shuttle, he was not taking any chances.

And then there was the Lamprey. He was squatting at the far end of the area, seemingly tireless, staring silently at Cord with bright, unblinking eyes.

At the side of the area, Samella was working with fierce concentration on one of GUIDE's disrupted memory banks. She had recovered now from the mysterious pain, but there were dark circles of fatigue and stress under her eyes. Yet the memory bank in her hands contained, she thought, data about Klydor, and she was anxious to restore it.

She'll have to finish soon, Cord thought, so she can sleep. And somehow I'll have to stay awake, to *let* her sleep. . . .

At that moment Samella stood up, stretching wearily. "That's the best I can do, GUIDE."

"Thank you for re-activating me," the computer's soft voice replied. "I can now supply data about the forest."

"Go ahead," Samella invited.

"The forest stretches over fifty-six square kilometres of one of Klydor's largest land masses..."

"Leave the geography," Samella broke in. "Tell us about the aliens, and the other creatures."

"The humanoids," GUIDE said imperturbably, "are Class 2G forest primitives, who could be said to be the 'servants' of the trees. The trees supply much of their food—hard-shelled fruit, gathered annually. And in return the humanoids tend the forest, planting and transplanting seedlings, removing other plant life and all dead trees. And they protect the trees from the large flesh-eating predators."

"The worm-things," Samella said.

"Correct," GUIDE replied. And he went on to describe the quiet lives of the forest people, among the shadows of the great trees. Quiet lives that were interrupted only when some of the worm-things— which were somnolent much of the time—awoke to feed. The monsters ate most flesh, GUIDE said, but found it easiest to feed on the brains of the trees.

"The *what?*" Cord asked.

"The growths on the trees are brains of a sort, and are sentient," GUIDE continued. ("It means they have minds of some kind," Samella interpreted.) "They can communicate with one another, and with the humanoids, so they will seek the humanoids' aid when the predators threaten them."

"It doesn't always do much good," Cord growled, realizing sickly that the monster which had attacked the leaning tree in the clearing had fed on the naked brain of a living creature with a mind.

The computer's soft voice continued, with some details about the other life forms they had seen. And it told them that the forest people had a metabolism ("how their bodies work," Samella had explained) close to a human's—as might be expected on an Earth-type planet. So any food and water they might find in the forest would not harm them.

That would have been good news, Cord thought dourly, before the alien attack. But it wouldn't be much use if they had to stay trapped in the shuttle.

Then, as GUIDE announced that he had no more direct data on the forest, Cord drifted off into sombre thought. Certainly they were trapped, now that the forest people had been roused into warlike fury. They could survive for a while on their own food and water supplies. But it would be a tense and miserable while, cooped up together—with the Lamprey waiting and watching, every moment. Maybe the aliens would get bored, he thought, and go away and leave them alone. And then they could simply move, leave the forest and wander the planet for a time. Though perhaps not until he and Samella had thought of a way to deal with the menace of the Lamprey. . . .

Those thoughts were still swirling through his tired mind some time later. The Lamprey had withdrawn into his private sleeping place, in the forward area, and Cord had been relieved to be free of that malevolent, hot-eyed glare. And Samella too was asleep, having first made Cord promise to wake her after a few hours, so that she could stand guard while he slept.

But he had privately decided not to keep that promise. With that agonizing headache, she had been through more than any of them, during the day. She needed a proper sleep—for it would be a disaster if she fell ill. Surely, Cord thought, I can keep awake just for one night.

He was still firmly telling himself that, as his heavy eyes drifted shut, and his head nodded slowly forward. . . .

It might have been a second or an hour later when he came awake with a huge spasmodic jerk. His eyes flew open—and adrenalin flashed through him like a flood of icy water.

The Lamprey towered over him, with a leering, triumphant grin. And the bony hands were aiming the laserifle at the centre of Cord's forehead.

"Knew you'd fall asleep," the vicious voice said. "You're nothing, MaKiy, a stupid kid. You thought you could handle an ex-Crusher, a Death Angel? You never had a chance."

Cord stared at the rifle, his face blank as stone. The maniac would surely kill him now, and then have Samella and the others at his mercy. All because he, Cord, was just what the Lamprey said. A stupid kid.

From across the area he heard Samella's sharp gasp, and Jeko's nervous hiss. But he did not take his eyes from the deadly muzzle.

"Any of the rest of you moves," the Lamprey snarled, "MaKiy gets it right away. Maybe I'll burn his legs off, let him crawl around awhile before he dies." A high, evil giggle. "But even that's too easy."

The bony hands moved on the rifle, and Cord saw part of the weapon pull free—a flat oblong of plastic, with jutting metal spikes. The Lamprey slid the oblong into his tunic pocket.

"That's the power pack, chub. Rifle's useless now." He turned, a twitch of blurring speed, and tossed the rifle to Jeko, who caught it automatically. "I'll want that back, when I'm done," the Lamprey snapped. "And the rest of you stay where you are. Anyone tries anything, they'll be next, when I'm finished with MaKiy."

Then he turned back to Cord, and bloodlust flamed in the mad eyes. "See, chub? No gun. And no backing down for you now. I'm going to take you apart, slow and painful, with my bare hands."

10
Defeat

No one in the area moved as Cord slowly stood up. But he was hardly aware of the others. He seemed to be looking down a narrow, focused tunnel, his gaze held by the Lamprey's glare, as if he were half-hypnotized.

He knew he could not escape this fight, now, even though he would not survive it if the Lamprey kept his murderous promise. He also knew that his strength would be of little use against the madman's combat skills. But all the same, Cord was not about to beg for mercy, or try to escape. This collision had been inevitable from the Lamprey's first appearance. So Cord gathered himself for battle, as emotionless and fatalistic as a gladiator from Earth's ancient days, going out to fight and die because it was all he could do.

And then the Lamprey sprang.

Cord saw him begin to move, and his hands went up to fend off the attack, and to grasp and

hold. But they clutched only empty air. And the
blow landed before he saw it coming.

It was like a sledge-hammer, high on the side of
his face. It rocked and staggered him, and bright
agony exploded in his skull. But though his eyes
blurred, he did not fall. His head had rolled with the
blow, the powerful muscles of his neck absorbing
some of the impact.

Even so, the Lamprey had hit him three more
times before he could recover his balance. And the
third blow was a crushing kick to the centre of
Cord's torso, hurling him back against the twisted
metal of the wall of the forward section.

But Cord was agile and athletic despite his solid
strength. Though he was half-stunned by that battering
kick, he managed to keep his feet and twist his body,
so that he merely grazed the edges of jagged metal
instead of falling heavily against them. As he straightened, lurching to one side, he heard a tearing sound—
but it was his tunic, not his flesh.

As the Lamprey stalked him, he ripped off the
torn tunic and flung it aside. And despite his knowledge that defeat and death were not far away, he felt
a small inner satisfaction at the flicker in the Lamprey's eyes. Not only was Cord still on his feet after
that first savage attack—but he was now revealed to
have scarcely a gram of fat on his body. Just hard
mounded muscle on chest and back, a flat ridged
stomach like armour, the rolling bulge of shoulders
and arms.

At least, Cord thought dourly, he might stop
calling me "chub".

Then the Lamprey leaped again, a pale blur of

motion. Cord swung up a hand to block another hammering punch, but it had been a feint. He felt his legs swept from under him by a slashing kick, and he fell painfully. But even so he was able to roll as he fell, so that the following kick merely glanced bruisingly off his hip.

Again he clambered to his feet, but only in time to receive a brutal, flashing chop to the side of his neck. Despite the cushion of muscle, the blow seemed to numb the left side of his body. He swung his right fist in a furious arc—but, giggling his mad laugh, the Lamprey slid under the punch, and the full murderousness of his fury poured over Cord like an avalanche.

Vicious blows and kicks landed so rapidly that it was as if Cord were fighting half a dozen Lampreys. He was flung away, crashing to the floor, and was struck again almost as he landed. He tried to roll, and was struck twice more before he began.

Half-unconscious, his body ablaze with pain, Cord wanted to curl into a ball and let himself slide into oblivion. But he would not let himself. Despite the storm of savagery, he kept struggling to regain his feet, kept trying to swing a half-blind and aimless fist, to keep the tormentor at bay.

For a moment he thought he had managed it, as the onslaught halted. He lurched to his knees, and only then registered a sound that he could not recognize.

It was the fizzing hiss of a laser beam biting into metal. And from what seemed a great distance, Cord heard Samella's raging voice.

"Move a finger and I'll cut you in half!" she cried.

For a chill instant there was total silence within the shuttle. And with the remnants of his strength, Cord shook his battered head and blinked to clear his vision.

Samella was standing, white-faced and wild-eyed, with the laserifle in her hands, pointing it at the Lamprey. And the madman was crouched, staring at her with eyes like fire, lips writhing in a grimace that was both grin and snarl.

"So you found where I stashed the spare power packs," the Lamprey said viciously. "But you won't shoot. You got no guts for killing."

The rifle muzzle shifted slightly. "I've got the guts to put holes in your knee-caps," Samella said. "And the accuracy." Her voice sounded almost as vicious as her opponent's.

The Lamprey's lean body tensed, like a snake coiling to strike. But the rifle did not waver, nor did Samella's eyes change. And something in her gaze was convincing enough even for the Lamprey's maddened blood-lust.

Some of the wildness left his eyes, and he straightened slightly. "You think you've saved MaKiy?" he asked coldly. "We're just back where we were before. 'Cept next time, I'll be aiming to kill *you*, sweets, along with him."

"There'll be no next time," Samella told him fiercely. "You have two choices, Lamprey. I can use this rifle to cripple you, so you can never hurt anyone again. Or you can walk out of that airlock, and keep walking."

The Lamprey's eyes widened. "Walk? Out?" he repeated blankly.

"Out," Samella said. "Get away from us and stay away. Take your chances with the aliens. Go live somewhere else. It's a big planet." Her knuckles grew white as she tightened her grip on the rifle. "If you show yourself near us again, you won't get a second chance."

The Lamprey's manic giggle rose. "Like I said, sweets, you got no guts. Sure, I'll walk away. I can get along out there just fine. But you *think*, sweets, and the rest of you blank-heads. Every day, every night, I'll be out there. You won't see me, but I'll be there. And sometime, maybe a week or a month from now, I'll be back. And you'll be dead 'fore you know I'm there—you and MaKiy and anyone else who sides with you."

"Burn him!" Heleth shouted suddenly, stepping forward. "He'll never just walk away! Kill him now, while you can!"

For an instant something cold and deadly glinted in Samella's grey eyes. But then she shook her head. "Maybe I should. But I'm no lunatic killer. This is our world now, where we have to live. We shouldn't have to start our life here in all the worst ways. What's happened already is bad enough—really *human*, all this hating and fighting and killing. I'm not adding cold-blooded murder to the list."

The Lamprey giggled. "Then you're a fool, sweets. You talk about your life here, but you got no life. ColSec will come along, a while from now, and all they'll find is the Lamprey—the only survivor." His evil grin flashed. "You're *dead*, sweets—all of you. Only you don't know it yet."

Slowly, mockingly, he stalked to the open airlock, and disappeared into the night.

The gun drooped in Samella's hands, and she swayed slightly with the release of the unbearable tension. But then she recovered herself, and glanced at Cord.

By then pain and exhaustion and shock had overcome him. He had sagged to the floor, and his battered, bleeding body had slid into unconsciousness.

"Heleth," Samella said quickly, "could you get some water and the medi-kit and see what you can do for Cord?" The dark girl nodded and hurried away, as Samella turned to the two Streeters. "Jeko, you and Rontal might drag a casket across the airlock. Just in case the Lamprey pays us a return visit tonight."

Jeko also nodded wordlessly and began to move. But Rontal stood rooted, looking at Samella with a faint frown.

"I don't like this," he said slowly.

Samella's hands tensed on the rifle. "What don't you like?" she asked sharply. "You taking the Lamprey's side?"

The tall boy blinked, startled. "No chance," he said quickly. "That freak-brain scared the light out of me from the start. And Jeko and me think you're right, that everythin' here has got started in the worst way. But the Lamprey, he's right too. He *is* gonna be out there. He'll wait a while, 'cause he likes to scare folk near as much as he likes to hurt. But he'll come after us."

Samella stared at him, surprised by the unexpectedly long speech. But then she shrugged tiredly. "Maybe he will," she said. "We'll just have to be on our guard."

"Every day, all day and night?" Rontal asked. "With only one gun? We got aliens out there who want to kill us, and a buggy ex-Crusher who wants to kill us, and prob'ly a whole bagful of things we haven't *met* yet that want to kill us." He shook his head gloomily. "That's what I don't like. We're gonna be scared all the time, jumping at shadows. No kind of way to live."

"Maybe one of those worm-things will eat old Lamprey," Jeko put in, forcing a laugh.

"More likely the other way round," Rontal growled.

Samella stared bleakly at the empty airlock, her eyes shadowed. "I know it shouldn't be like this, Rontal. But it is. So we just have to live one day at a time. Starting with tomorrow."

"Sure," Rontal said, with a deep sigh. "But I just keep wonderin' how many tomorrows we got left."

11

The Screaming

Three days later, to his own surprise, Cord was nearly recovered from the fearsome beating. His injuries had proved to be mostly superficial. His healthy solidity of muscle and bone had saved him from any fractures or dislocations, so he had suffered only cuts and grazes, along with plenty of bruises and a few strained tendons. Parts of his body still ached, but the blackness of his bruises was beginning to fade, and he was rapidly regaining normal fitness.

But if his body was improving, his state of mind was not. And the others seemed just as troubled and tense—because they were all living with the strain of being in a permanent state of siege.

The forest people were still prowling through the forest beyond the edge of the clearing. Day and night they were there, sometimes fifty or more of them, never fewer than thirty. Now and then some of them would step out into the clearing, to stare briefly at the shuttle, fangs bared and leaf-blades raised, before slipping back into the forest shadows. At other times they would be invisible, even to Heleth's night vision, but occasional growls or angry feline shrieks would reveal their continuing presence.

And the Lamprey, too, was out there somewhere. He had obviously managed to melt away into the darkness unseen, when Samella had driven him from the shuttle, for there had been no alien outcry or pursuit. And though Cord found himself half-hoping that the Lamprey might fall foul of the savage forest beings, he suspected that the madman's skills in wild country would probably keep him safe from harm. Meanwhile, that last evil threat of the Lamprey's seemed to remain in the very air within the shuttle, like a dark and stifling shadow.

So the five of them spent those days simply moping, mostly in a glum silence, staring out of the airlock at the gloomy and unwelcoming forest, or simply staring into nothingness, dreaming miserable dreams of what they might have been doing back on Earth.

But when Cord began to feel better, he whiled away some of the third day by using one of the sharp metal fragments, from the wreckage, to trim the length of tree-root that he had wielded against the aliens. Soon he had made it into a solid club, with a bulky, rounded head and sturdy haft. And the spirits of the others lifted a little, when Cord's club inspired them to make weapons of their own.

Heleth and the Streeters risked a brief venture into the clearing—the aliens came out and stared, but did not attack—to gather some broken lengths of young trees, no more than saplings. Back in the shuttle, they split the ends, inserted narrow, sharp-pointed metal shards, and bound the ends with strips of tough cloth from the padding of a casket. The result was three serviceable spears—to which they added crude knives, by wrapping more cloth around one end of three more tapering splinters of metal.

The weapons cheered them up considerably, even when Samella grinned at them teasingly. "You're not even a barbarian now," she told Cord. "You're a primitive. All of you—all of *us*. We're sinking fast."

"At least we're still dressed like civilized folk," Cord replied. Some extra clothing had also been found among the supplies they had salvaged, so he had been able to replace his torn tunic.

"You call this *dressed?*" Heleth grumbled, plucking at one sleeve of her muddy-brown uniform. "I think ColSec could've left us our own clothes."

That led to a rowdy discussion of the merits of the various styles of dress, which seemed to Cord unbelievably weird, among the gangs of Limbo and the Bunkers. As it went on, Cord's thoughts drifted away. Heleth's mention of ColSec had stirred something at the back of his mind, a half-memory that he could not quite grasp. It might have been just his continuing anger, that unending flame of hatred that burned within him for the ruthless organization that had exiled them all in this threatening alien forest. But somehow he thought it was more than that. . . .

He brooded for the rest of the day, worrying about it even through another dreary meal of food concentrate. And then, at last, that evening, it came to him.

"Samella," he said urgently, "I've just thought

of something. When the Lamprey first arrived, he said something about ColSec coming here, after a while. What did he mean?"

Rontal snapped his fingers. "Right! He said it again, when Samella chased him out. I clean forgot!"

"So did I," Samella said, frowning. "But I don't know what he meant. GUIDE, can you explain?"

"Colonization Section operating procedure," the computer's soft voice told them, "provides for an inspection team to be sent after six months, to learn whether the first colonists have survived, and whether the colony has discovered resources or materials of value."

Rontal's face darkened. "That's *all* we need. Prob'ly bring a bunch of CeeDees with them."

"But we crashed," Cord said thoughtfully. "Won't they think we're all dead?"

"There are no communications links with colonial shuttles," GUIDE said. "Inspection teams are sent automatically, after the required time."

"Even when the freighter doesn't get to where it was going?" Cord persisted. "When they know that it's lost, they'll think we were lost with it."

"The freighter would not have reached its destination," GUIDE said, "for another eight months. By then, the inspection team will be here."

Jeko tossed his empty food container aside, petulantly. "They can come sooner, far as I'm concerned. Might bring us somethin' worth eatin'."

Cord glared at him. "Is that all you can think of? When they sling us out here not caring if we live or die, and then come along to see if we've found anything to make them richer?"

"Cord, don't," Samella broke in quickly, as Jeko drew back abashed. "ColSec isn't our problem *now*. We have to think of some way to get out of this fix." She looked around at them all sternly. "Even if we could face the thought of spending six months inside here, waiting for ColSec to come and rescue us, that won't happen. Because the food supplies we have won't *last* that long."

Rontal grunted. "Maybe the Lamprey was right. Maybe he *is* gonna be the only survivor."

A long, sombre silence followed that remark. And then the silence was shattered—from outside.

Across the darkened clearing, from the forest's edge, they heard an outburst of the savage, yowling cries of the forest people.

Samella snatched up the laserifle and leaped to the airlock, with Cord at her side, club in hand, and the others crowding after. And this time they did not need Heleth's night vision to show them what was happening.

A group of the aliens, about thirty of them as usual, were pouring out into the clearing, their leaf-blade weapons glinting in the starlight.

Samella half-lifted the rifle to her shoulder—and then lowered it again. The beings were clearly not attacking the shuttle. Their charge was angled in a different direction—along the edge of the clearing, towards a particularly tall and bulky tree.

And then Cord and the others saw it. The long, solid shape of a huge worm-thing, sliding swiftly and silently over the turf towards the same tree.

The monster was not nearly as big as the gigantic, motionless hillock that they had seen in the forest, during their exploration. But it was big enough. It seemed nearly four metres long, and the top of its turf-covered back would be as high, Cord guessed, as his own waist. As the aliens drew near, it halted its rapid slither and reared up, its head rising higher than the tallest alien, the tentacles around its mouth snapping and lashing like thick, heavy rope.

Yet as before the forest people did not hesitate. Their leaf-blades seemed puny and useless, yet they hurled themselves at the monster, stabbing and slashing. But few of those glittering weapons found their marks—because the tentacles were finding theirs. The vicious, poisoned barbs sank into the flesh, and tore free, and suddenly ten of the aliens were crumpling, their bodies gripped by the strange convulsions.

The other twenty drew back for an instant, screeching. And the monstrous worm, still with its deadly head lifted in its defensive posture, slid rapidly forward to the base of the tall tree. Again the aliens leaped forward, in another suicidal attack, and again half a dozen of them fell under the ghastly counter-attack of the barbed tentacles.

The five young humans stared, silenced and chilled by the grim ferocity of the battle. And then, as the huge worm turned away from its remaining attackers and began oozing up the trunk of the tree, Cord heard Samella whimper.

He whirled, and saw with icy shock that she had stepped to the very edge of the airlock. Her eyes were wide and blank, her face twisted in agony. And she was muttering, in a voice almost too low to be heard.

"Stop it . . . the screaming . . . stop it. . . ."

Cord was mystified. The surviving aliens were shrieking and howling, but Cord could not understand why that noise should cause Samella such pain. He reached out to take her arm, to draw her back inside the shuttle.

But before he could reach her, she moved forward, leaping down on to the turf. Her face was stark white, her eyes were huge empty pools. And she dashed forward, with a chilling scream.

"Stop it! *Stop it!*"

She had not let go of the laserifle, and now she swung it up and fired. As the beam struck, a tongue of flame burst from the turf on the monster's back. The remaining aliens shrieked in terror, backing away rapidly towards the forest. But the worm kept climbing—slowly, because of its great weight, but unharmed.

Samella's cries had become wordless and hysterical as she fired again and again, wildly, at the impervious armour of the worm's shell. But then Cord and the others had caught up with her. Ignoring the retreating aliens, Cord jerked the rifle from her hands and thrust her towards Rontal, who was closest.

"Take her inside," he said.

"What you goin' to do?" Rontal asked.

"It seems to matter to Samella that the thing gets stopped," Cord said grimly. "So I'm going to try to stop it." He handed the rifle to Heleth. "Come on," he said to her and Jeko. "I'll need you."

The monstrous worm was still less than two metres from the ground, climbing slowly, when Cord reached the tree. He halted, taking a firm grip on his club. Then he set himself, and crashed the club against the side of the monster with all the power of his right arm.

For all the creature's bulk, the blow jolted it. It seemed to hesitate, and slip a little, and Cord swung the club in a second thunderous blow.

That one jolted the huge worm even more. Aware that it was being attacked, it reared partly up, and twisted, the hooked tentacles sweeping and flailing through the air, striving to reach down to find the flesh of its attacker. But Cord was just far enough below it to be safe. And revulsion added extra strength to his arm as he swung his club again, thundering it against the worm like a pile-driver.

And because the monster was partly reared up, so that only some of the small claws on its underside gripped the tree, the awesome force of that blow jolted it loose—and it fell.

It thumped to the ground on its armoured back, and at once reared up, unharmed. Its deadly tentacles lashed out as it slithered swiftly forward, so that Cord had to leap hastily back. But then Heleth sprang up beside him, and poured the full fury of the laser beam into the worm's gaping, unprotected mouth.

The forward slither halted. The mouth opened, closed, opened again, the tentacles writhing furiously. But as Heleth continued to fire, the huge armoured body sagged, collapsing to the ground, the tendrils drooping into the limp stillness of death.

Instantly Heleth whirled, rifle ready. The aliens had gone silent during Cord's battle with the worm, but as it died a wave of muttering growls had swept through them. And they were standing no more than twenty metres away from the three humans, leaf-blades raised.

Jeko, primitive spear in hand, moved up to stand beside Heleth and Cord. For a moment that seemed an age, the two groups stared at each other in silence.

"C'mon, then, saucer-eyes," Jeko muttered, "if you're comin'."

"Maybe they won't attack," Cord said quietly. "Back away slowly and see what happens."

They did as he said, moving warily back towards the shuttle. The dark, stooped alien figures stirred at the movement—and then, suddenly, they were no longer there. They too had backed away, vanishing soundlessly into the forest darkness.

Jeko released his breath in a sigh. "Everybody gets into the action 'cept me."

"You could chase after them," Heleth suggested.

"Some other time," Jeko said with a grin. He glanced around curiously at the huge, still form of the dead worm, and nudged Cord. "What say we cut ourselves a coupla steaks?"

"Yeck," Heleth said distastefully, and turned sharply away towards the shuttle. Laughing, Cord and Jeko hurried after her.

But their laughter vanished when they entered the shuttle. Samella was crouched miserably on the floor next to GUIDE's console, with Rontal hovering nearby, looking troubled.

"We stopped it," Cord said. "It's dead."

Samella lifted her tear-stained face. "Thank you," she whispered.

Cord gestured vaguely, as if to brush the thanks aside. "Samella, we have to figure this out. I mean . . . what's wrong with you, and if we can do something about it."

Samella turned away. "I think I know what's wrong with me," she said wretchedly. "GUIDE has a theory, and it must be right. And, Cord—" fresh tears sprang to her eyes—"it scares me half to death!"

12
Moving On

As Cord watched her anxiously, Samella explained.

"When Rontal brought me back inside," she said, "I was really frightened. I felt I was sick in some way—mentally. I wondered if the space-flight, and being in suspended animation, had messed my mind up somehow. But then I thought, if that was true, I'd feel the same way *inside* the shuttle. And I don't."

"Anyway, being in the caskets didn't hurt any of us," Heleth commented.

"'Cept maybe the Lamprey," Jeko muttered. "And he was buggy to start with."

"So," Samella went on, hardly hearing them, "I decided to ask GUIDE, if he could think of a reason why being outside, here, bothers me. I gave him the standard instruction—to set accuracy aside and give me a theory. A high-probability hypothesis. And he came up with something that *must* be the answer."

"What?" Cord and Heleth said together.

"He said... it's the *trees.*"

The others stared as Samella paused, gulped, and went on.

"GUIDE said that the trees probably communicate by *telepathy*, mind to mind. And he said that I probably have a... a 'moderate-level ESP receptive capability'."

"A what?" Cord asked blankly.

"It means I could be picking up things from the trees' minds. Like a receiver, picking up broadcasts. I wouldn't understand the meanings, or the language, if they even have one. But I can receive the *feelings* that the trees give out. Especially... the strongest ones."

Cord looked shocked. "So when you're in so much pain, and saying things about screaming..."

Samella nodded miserably. "Just about the worst time was at the beginning. The shuttle's crash had left all those hundreds of crushed and broken trees, and the whole forest was screaming. As if every tree was feeling the terrible pain, all that dying. And the forest also felt fear, and hatred, aimed at us—the killers."

"And you picked all that up," Cord said wonderingly.

"I suppose I'm lucky my mind didn't crack up," Samella said. "And every time we went out, later, I was affected. Not always as strongly, but the trees still felt fear and hate whenever we appeared."

"But inside the shuttle," Rontal put in, "seems the metal of the hull acts as a kind of *screen*, or something. So the trees can't get at her mind. That's what GUIDE says."

"And the worm-things..." Cord began.

"Same thing," Samella said. "When those monsters come out of their sleep, their somnolence, and go looking for food, the forest panics. Because any tree could be the victim. So they scream out their fear, and call the aliens to help them."

"Like tonight," Cord said slowly.

"Maybe they'll figure we're on their side now," Rontal said hopefully.

"After what the Lamprey did, and the fight we had with them?" Cord asked. "They'll take a lot of convincing."

"But this ESP stuff," Heleth said suddenly. "It's spooky. I mean—can you read minds? *Our* minds?"

Samella shook her head wearily. "Of course not. I'd have to have some conscious control of it. GUIDE's theory just says I'm a bit *receptive*. I pick up things now and then, without intending to. Especially the trees' pain and fear, because it's so powerful." She shuddered slightly.

"But *just* the trees?" Heleth persisted.

"I don't know . . . ." Samella frowned thoughtfully. "When I was a kid, sometimes I seemed to know what some people were going to say or do before it happened. And then the *dreams*. . . . In the casket, I had weird dreams of places and people I'd never seen. Limbo, the Bunkers, even the Highlands . . . And when all of you have talked about where you come from, it was just like I dreamed—every detail. So somehow I must have been picking up *your* dreams!"

The others looked at each other uneasily. "So you *can* pick up stuff from our heads," Rontal growled.

"Maybe, sometimes," Samella said unhappily. "But I can't help it—and I don't *want* to." She

brightened slightly. "But I haven't picked up anything from you since we got here, not even dreams.
So maybe it had something to do with the suspended
animation, when your dreams were stronger, and I
was *more* receptive."

The others looked a little relieved at that, and
Heleth nodded. "That makes sense..."

"Anyway, what's it matter?" Jeko cut in abruptly.
"So you got this ESP thing. Fine. Doesn't do any-
body any harm—'cept *you*. 'Cause the trees are
gonna come knockin' at your head every time you go
out." His mouth twisted bitterly. " 'Cept you *can't* go
out, and us neither. The aliens're gonna keep us
penned in here till we starve to death."

"No," Cord said flatly. "We'll move."

The others looked at him, startled.

"It's all we can do," Cord went on. "Get ourselves away from the aliens, and the Lamprey, and
the trees. Find ourselves another part of the planet
to live in."

"And maybe find somethin' worse than we got
here," Jeko said glumly.

"Or something better," Cord told him. "We
won't know till we try."

"The aliens're gonna jump us," Rontal pointed
out, "soon as we step outa here."

Cord shrugged. "Maybe. But we've got weapons
now, and they're afraid of the laserifle. We'll just
have to fight our way out. One way or another, we
have to leave."

The two Streeters grinned, not at all troubled
by the prospect of battle. But Heleth sighed heavily,

and wandered away to stare glumly out of the airlock. "Seems there should be something..." she began.

But then she stiffened, staring more tensely out at the night. And there was a strange excitement in her voice.

"Hey," she said. "Come and look!"

The others crowded up beside her, and peered out. They saw little in the darkness—only the vague shapes of the trees beyond the clearing, where the faint starlight outlined the rise of the leaf-branches. So they looked questioningly at Heleth, waiting to be told what her uncanny night vision had seen in the blackness.

And they saw that she was grinning delightedly.

"The aliens," she told them. "They're gone!"

It was difficult for Cord to restrain himself, and the others, from rushing out into the night and making sure. But though Heleth assured them that she could see no sign of the ominously watchful humanoid forms, they all realized that the forest beings might simply have withdrawn a short distance, just far enough to be out of range even of Heleth's cat-eyes.

"They *could* have gone away, though," Samella said hopefully. "After the fight with the worm. Maybe they don't see us as enemies any more."

"Or maybe they got business somewhere else," Jeko said with a laugh. "Like chasin' the Lamprey—if we're lucky."

"We'll find out in the morning," Cord said. "And if they *have* gone, it'll give *us* the chance to go. So we have to be ready to move."

Those words spurred the group into activity.

They gathered up everything that they had salvaged from the wreck—the remaining food and water, the medi-kit and tools, the spare parts for the laserifle, anything that might be useful. Then they busied themselves with strips of the tough cloth from the caskets, making containers for their possessions, to be slung over their shoulders like crude backpacks.

"And we have to take GUIDE," Samella said suddenly.

"Could slow us down," Cord said, frowning.

Samella smiled. "We won't take the console— and GUIDE himself is quite small. He'll fit in one of those." She gestured at the makeshift backpacks. "And he has his own power source, solar batteries that recharge from sunlight. I'll carry him myself, if you like."

"C'mon, muscles," Jeko said to Cord with a grin, "carry the lady's bag for her."

"All right," Cord said, laughing along with the others. "I suppose we can handle GUIDE, since we don't have that much to carry. Just as long as everything is ready by first light."

Jeko groaned. "So early? Seems nobody's gonna get any sleep around here."

But in fact they did all get some sleep that night, once all their supplies had been packed away, and after Samella had carefully removed GUIDE from the console and placed him, with his batteries, in one of the backpacks. And even Jeko rose eagerly, when the first misty grey of dawn showed itself in the clearing outside, and went out with the others to see whether the siege really had been lifted, whether the forest beings were really no longer waiting and watching among the trees.

And in less than an hour they found that Heleth had been right. They moved warily more than half a kilometre in among the trees, and then turned to make a complete circle all around the clearing. And they saw nothing except the trees, and the misty, shadowy, empty spaces between them.

"Wonder where they've got to?" Rontal said.

"We'll probably never know," Cord said. "But at least we've got our chance to start moving."

"All right," Samella said cheerily. "Let's pick up our things, and go find a way out of the woods."

13

Heart of the Forest

"One direction is as good as another," Cord said, "when you don't know where you're starting from."

They were standing at one end of the clearing, looking out along the sweep of the open corridor that had been slashed through the forest by the shuttle's sliding crash. Cord had decided to start out along the corridor, because at least it offered them some safety, in its openness, from an ambush that might possibly await them in the shadowed forest.

So, after glancing back once more at the silent, crumpled wreck of the shuttle, they had set out— cheerful and determined—to take their first steps in the exploration of their new world.

But shortly, as they moved forward along the broad open path, the orange sun rose, bright and warm. And Heleth began to blink and grumble, which made Rontal nudge Jeko.

"We're gonna have to find a place with a nice

dark cave for this Bunkers gal," he said with a grin. "She's about as happy in the sun as a *real* vampire."

Heleth glowered. "Sun doesn't bother me," she said unconvincingly. "Shade's better, that's all."

But Cord was more concerned about Samella's feelings, just then. Since they had left the shuttle he had seen the small frown lines between her eyes, the slight tension around her mouth. "Is your head all right?" he asked at last.

"It's not bad," she assured him. "Not like before. Just a strange kind of pressure—a feeling of being watched. I can put up with it."

Cord nodded, feeling a faint chill at the eeriness of the uncanny mental link between Samella and the trees. But it won't be for long, he told himself. And at least *he* had no sense of being watched, no feeling of threatening alien eyes fixed on him from the forest shadows. Even so, he kept a careful watch on the trees at either side of the broad trail—and saw that Heleth and the two Streeters, warrior instincts alert, were doing just the same.

And it was not only aliens that they were watching for.

"One thing I don't like," Heleth said after a few more minutes of walking. "That freaky Lamprey out here somewhere. What if he follows us, wherever we go?"

"We still got the rifle," Rontal growled. "If he shows up and tries somethin'... then we make sure he doesn't show up again."

"The aliens've prob'ly got him by now," Jeko said lightly.

"He's a Crusher," Heleth reminded them. "He can probably handle the aliens all by himself."

"Forget him," Cord said firmly. "He probably won't follow us—and if he does, we'll worry about it then."

The others shrugged, nodded, and began chatting about other matters. And again Cord felt slightly uneasy at this ready acceptance of his decisions, his leadership. But since that was the way they seemed to prefer it, he knew he would have to put up with it. For now.

At the same time, he felt a renewed pleasure at the friendship, the easy closeness, that was growing so rapidly among the oddly mixed five of them. One thing to thank the Lamprey for, he thought dourly, and the aliens. Having common enemies, being in danger together, had bound them together faster than anything else could have done.

But at least there seemed to be no danger threatening them at that moment. And so they forged ahead, keeping up a brisk and energetic pace despite the clumsy packs on their backs. Until, a little more than an hour after the sun had risen, they reached the end of the path that the shuttle's crash had cleared. They paused there for a moment, staring ahead into the forest dimness that awaited them on all sides.

"At least we get some shade now," Heleth said happily.

"Right," Jeko said. "Shade, and aliens, and worm-things, and the Lamprey..."

Still, they had no choice. So they set off into the shadowed depths, even more tense and watchful than before. But after another kilometre, it was not the aliens or any other enemy that stopped them. It was the fact that Samella's pace was slowing, and stumbling now and then, and her face was pale and her teeth clenched.

"Should I take your pack for a while?" Cord asked at last, looking concerned.

Samella shook her head painfully. "It's not that. It's the trees... They're getting worse, like before. I can feel the hate and fear, pouring out...."

"What's up with them?" Rontal wondered, glancing uneasily around. "We're not doing anything."

Heleth frowned. "Could be we're heading somewhere they don't want us to be."

"You don't reckon they're sorry to see us goin'?" Jeko said, forcing a smile.

But Cord was nodding thoughtfully. "Heleth could be right. Maybe it's the direction we're going." He stared ahead at the unchanging forest depths. "We could split up, for a while," he said at last. "One of us could stay behind, with Samella, and the other three could keep going a little way, and see what's up ahead."

"I don't know," Samella said doubtfully.

"It's the best way," Cord insisted. "You and Heleth could take the rifle and go back to the clear area, where the pain wasn't so bad for you. And the three of us could keep going, just for a while. We'll be all right. We haven't seen an alien all morning—and if we do, we'll just run for it."

Samella still looked doubtful, but Heleth was glaring. "You want us *girls* to go back," she said angrily, "while the big brave *men* go exploring?"

"Right," Jeko said with a snicker. "And you *girls* can get some eats ready for when us men get back."

Heleth turned her glare on him. "You big-mouthed Streeter yeck," she snapped, "I say *you* stay behind—or I break your skinny back."

Jeko's eyes narrowed, and he started forward. But he stopped as if he had run into a wall when Cord slapped a brawny arm across his chest.

"Stop it," Cord said sternly. "Remember what Samella said, when she drove the Lamprey out. We want no more fighting—not among ourselves."

Jeko subsided, glowering. "Maybe so. But maybe some of us gotta watch what we say."

"That's a true thing," Heleth told him. "For *all* of us."

"Seems fair," Rontal put in. "You did kinda push her, Jeko."

Jeko glanced at him, then suddenly smiled, looking a little shamefaced. "Right enough. I'll say sorry."

"And me," Heleth said, returning the smile. "But I still say I'm going exploring."

Jeko's smile widened. "You got it, Bunker lady. Your eyes are better'n mine anyway."

Cord let his breath out slowly, feeling relieved and cheered. It seemed that their friendship was strong enough to withstand a flare of anger, even among these wild, street-fighting kids. Maybe, he thought, there's hope for us yet, on Klydor.

But not, he added dourly, if we don't get out of this forest fairly soon.

So the group separated. Samella, still dubious but also grateful, turned back with Jeko towards the open clearing, where the mental pain from the trees had affected her far less. And Cord led the other two forward, deeper into the forest.

They had been watchful before, but now their nervous wariness increased with each step they took. Since Samella had the laserifle, they would be in far more danger if they met a group of the blade-wielding forest beings, or another of the larger-sized worm-things. One club and two spears would not be weaponry enough, they knew, in such an encounter. So as they moved ahead, there was hardly a single shadowed tree-trunk, hardly a single bulge in the springy turf, that they did not study with edgy caution before passing near to it.

But after they had travelled for several kilometres, with not the slightest sign of danger or threat, the knots in Cord's nerves began to unravel slightly. And he cheered up even more when he glimpsed, in the distance ahead, a wide brightness—which could only be sunlight, pouring down, unhindered by the dense leaf-branches.

The edge of the forest, he thought exultantly.

The three of them ran eagerly forward. But when they broke out into the open, they halted, with a mixture of feelings. They were disappointed, because they found themselves not in open country but simply in a large clearing, about half a kilometre across, with the forest looming all around. But they also felt amazement—because the clearing was not empty.

In its centre stood one tree. And it was simply the hugest living thing Cord had ever seen.

The tree was not unusually tall, not much more than thirty metres from the ground. But its girth was stupendous. The enormous bulk of its trunk, creased and scarred with age, stood like a mighty tower. From the top, a high fan of leaf-branches rose up another ten or fifteen metres. And within that fan, crowning the enormity of the trunk, they could see the tree's "brain", a vast wrinkled bulge that loomed like some mountain promontory.

"Now that," Rontal said softly, "is a *tree!*"

Cord stepped forward, his club ready. Something seemed to be twined around the gigantic trunk, near the ground—looking like a snake of some sort, or perhaps just a vine. But as he drew closer, Cord saw that it was a kind of rope, thick and strong, looking like it had been woven or plaited out of thin strips of some animal hide. And though he had no idea why it should be there, girdling the colossal tree, he felt the hairs on his neck bristle with a nameless fear.

Beside him, Heleth halted, clearly feeling the same way. "I don't like this," she said uneasily.

Rontal, another time, might have teased her again about her dislike of sunlight and open sky. But this time he merely nodded. "That tree's just *too* big," he said. "Spooky."

The words seemed to focus Cord's thoughts, as he gazed at the enormous tree. And realization struck him.

"It's not the size of it," he said slowly. "We don't like this place because *it* doesn't like *us*. And this tree's so big, with such a powerful brain, that even *we* can feel some of the fear and hate it's sending out." His voice tightened. "This is why Samella was getting worse, the closer she got to this place. Imagine what she'd be feeling if she'd come this far."

Heleth grimaced. "Let's move."

"We better," Rontal agreed. "Maybe this tree's callin' a bunch of aliens to come and get rid of us." He glanced up, forcing a nervous grin. "We're goin' now, tree," he called. "We're not gonna hurt you, or any tree—no more. Okay?"

The others laughed, half-heartedly, and moved swiftly across the clearing, to plunge back into the forest. As before, they maintained their careful, edgy watch on the shadows around them. Within a few minutes, the sense of fear and threat that they had felt in the clearing began to wane. And still there was no sign of the forest beings.

"Wonder where the aliens are?" Heleth said idly after a few more moments of watchful travel.

"A long way from here, I hope," Cord said.

"Maybe chasin' the Lamprey somewhere," Rontal said with a chuckle, "like Jeko said."

And good luck to them, Cord thought grimly. He glanced up at the sky, and saw that it was just about midday. "Let's hurry along," he told the others. "We'll pick up Samella and Jeko, eat something, and be on our way. Samella should be all right if we stay well away from that big tree."

But, back in the open area at that moment, Samella was far from all right.

When she and Jeko had emerged from the trees into the open corridor, she had felt much better. The torment in her mind had eased to nothing more than a dull headache. And so she had begun to while away the time by unpacking a few micro-tools, and working on one of the memory banks of GUIDE—who was, after all, in her backpack. And Jeko had taken charge of the laserifle, and was lounging next to her, chatting idly.

Now and then he would peer intently around, at the silent forest that stood on either side of them. But, sitting in bright sunlight, it was impossible for him to see very deeply into the dim depths among the trees. So there was no chance that he could have seen the flickering movement within those depths—a movement like a darting, flitting shadow, pale and silent as a wraith.

The pale shadow reached the edge of the open corridor, still unseen, and slid behind the broad trunk of one of the larger trees. And there it seemed to vanish, as if the ground had swallowed it up.

Time passed, and Samella continued to concentrate on her work. And Jeko began to grow bored, and restless. He rose and began to wander around the open area, pausing now and then to peer into the forest. Hefting the rifle, he was almost hoping that some aliens would show themselves, if only to provide a little excitement.

Then his eyes narrowed. He had seen a tiny, flapping movement, on the side of one of the larger trees at the edge of the area. Probably one of the blue flying things, he thought. Grinning, he ambled over towards the tree, vaguely planning to catch the creature, and present it to Heleth as her midday meal.

He did not see the pale, lean shape lurking in the shadow on the other side of the bulky tree-trunk, as he approached. Nor did he see, in time, the long arm that flashed out like a striking snake towards him.

Samella had been paying no attention to Jeko's restless wanderings, but she looked up with annoyance as a shadow fell across her lap, and the delicate computer connection she was making.

The annoyance turned instantly to a frightened gasp.

Several paces away, Jeko was slumped on hands and knees, looking half-stunned. And above Samella stood a white-haired, hot-eyed apparition, with the laserifle gripped in one bony hand.

"Told you I'd be back, sweets," the Lamprey said, with a grin of pure savagery. "And when I'm done with the little blank-head, there—it'll be your turn!"

14

The Search

Cord had led the others away from the clearing with the giant tree by a different route—curving deeper into the forest to be sure that no other obstacles would block their path when they passed that way again, with Jeko and Samella. They had travelled only about a kilometre farther when they came to another clearing. But this one held no lone tree. It held no living things at all.

They saw a huge number of dead trees, stacked carefully in intricate patterns. The leaf-branches had all been removed, and were piled at the edge of the clearing. Some of the trees, lower in the stacks, had obviously been dead a long time, and were decayed and crumbling. But others, those piled on top, seemed freshly dead—and many of the trunks were broken and splintered.

"It's a . . . a graveyard!" Heleth said abruptly.

"That's it," Cord agreed. "This must be where

the aliens brought the smashed trees from our clearing. And all other dead trees, I suppose."

"Like the ones killed by worm-things," Rontal added. "So that's why we don't see dead trees in the forest."

Cord nodded absently. He had noticed that the brain-growths had also been removed from the stacked trunks. But he could see no sign of them. Then Rontal, who had moved warily into the clearing, beckoned to the others. And when they joined him, they saw a broad stretch of freshly turned earth at the clearing's centre.

"You reckon they bury the brains of dead trees?" Rontal asked.

"Must be," Heleth said. "Maybe so those monsters don't get them."

"Looks like *something's* been trying to get them," Cord said.

They saw what he was looking at—a small patch of the fresh earth that had been disturbed, dug into as if by some burrowing creature.

"Can worm-things dig, d'you think?" Heleth wondered. But then she paused—for Cord had stiffened, then crouched to peer closely at the ground.

A mark in the soft earth, next to the shallow hole that had been dug. A clear, deep footprint— made by a booted foot.

"The Lamprey," Cord said grimly, straightening up. "It was probably him that was digging."

"Just like him," Rontal muttered, "to disturb the dead. . . ."

Cord moved away, searching the turf around the patch of bare earth. The signs were there, though not easy to see—some slightly crushed turf, another faint imprint of a boot-heel. Rontal and Heleth were impressed, for they could hardly see the signs when Cord pointed them out. But they were clear enough to Cord, who had stalked red deer and other creatures all his life. And a few metres away from the stacks of trees, on the edge of the clearing, there was a sign that was clear to all of them.

The remains of a fire. And a few small bones of some creature—perhaps one of the furry waddlers.

"He wasn't lying when he said he could live in the wild," Cord said dourly. "Went off bare-handed, but he's hunting, making a fire...."

"He must be burning the trees!" Heleth said, looking shocked. "The splintered ones—from the graveyard!"

"That's not goin' to make those aliens any happier with us," Rontal growled.

Cord bent and touched the ashes, finding a faint warmth at their depths. "He might have been here last night, or early this morning."

"And maybe not so far away now," Rontal said.

Cord rose, scanning the forest around them. It could well be, he thought, that the Lamprey was crouched nearby, watching them. But Cord felt that, if so, he would sense it—would somehow *feel* those glittering eyes on him.

"No telling where he is," he said at last. He glanced up at the sun again. "Let's go. We're losing time."

"Any time," Heleth said fervently. "It's getting a little creepy around here."

So they set off on the return journey—still

keeping up their swift pace, still maintaining a careful watch on the forest gloom around them. Kilometre after kilometre, they moved steadily on, rarely speaking now, each wrapped in private and troubled thoughts.

Cord was feeling increasingly uneasy. He had no wish to meet the Lamprey, but he would have liked to know just where the madman was, at that moment. For the hundredth time, he told himself there was nothing to worry about. Not with Jeko standing guard with the laserifle. And he knew he had been right to leave Samella behind, not exposing her to the pain from that monster tree in the clearing.

But all the same, the uneasiness grew within him, until he had to struggle against the urge to break into a run. And from the grim silence of the others, he sensed that they felt the same way. So they hurried on, anxious and determined.

Until the moment when their path was barred—when sheer horror loomed out of the shadows towards them.

It was a gigantic worm—one that would have dwarfed even the huge one they had killed the night before. The vast body stretched nearly fifteen metres along the ground, and the turf-covered, armoured back rose two metres from the ground. As it slithered among the trees towards them, it looked like an ancient, weathered hilltop on the move.

"It's the one we saw before—that Jeko climbed on!" Heleth said, wide-eyed.

"Only it woke up," Rontal growled.

The monster sensed their presence, and its front end reared up menacingly. The mouth gaped wide, like some ghastly cavern in a horror dream. And the tentacles around it were like lengths of the stoutest cable, with the hooks on the ends as large and evilly sharp as the barbs on a harpoon, and stained purplish-green with the deadly venom.

Then it flexed its titanic body, and flung itself forward at its prey.

For all its ponderous bulk, it moved with amazing speed. The three young humans were barely able to hurl themselves aside as the ghastly head struck at them, the barbed tentacles whistling as they flashed through the air. Then the monster gathered itself, rearing even higher, and charged again.

Cord and the others had split up, in their first desperate scramble for safety, and it was Rontal alone that the monster slithered towards in its second charge. The tall Streeter sprang away, then glanced back—just in time to fling his spear up and ward off a huge, dripping, tentacled hook that had been slashing down at his back.

But then Rontal dodged between two trees growing fairly close together. The giant worm, moving at its full speed, slammed into the narrow gap—and found that it was too vast to force itself through. For a moment it seemed to be stuck, as it fought to reverse direction, tentacles flailing wildly. And in that moment the three humans leaped away in a frantic, headlong dash. They were a quarter of a kilometre away before they looked back, in time to see that the gigantic creature had given up the chase, and was slithering away in the opposite direction.

"I'm gonna be *glad* to get out of this place," Rontal said fervently.

"One thing," Heleth said, "that worm's too big to climb trees."

"It wouldn't need to," Cord said. "It could just push them over." He paused, as a thought struck him. "Though there's *one* tree it might climb. . . ."

The others looked startled as they followed his thought. "The biggest worm-thing, and the biggest tree. . . ." Heleth said slowly. "And remember that rope around the big tree. . . ?"

"I was thinking about that," Cord replied. "If the trees are special to the aliens, then the biggest tree must be most special. So the aliens must have to be *sure* to protect it, from the worms."

The others nodded uneasily. "You think they tie somethin' to the big tree," Rontal said, "so a worm would eat that, 'stead of the tree's brain?"

"Could be," Cord said. He was silent for a moment, feeling a strange uneasy chill. But then he shook himself. "It's not our problem. We've got enough to worry about."

Once again they set off at their steady pace, and the kilometres began to unroll behind them. And Cord's uneasiness grew no less. If anything, it began to grow into a sense of foreboding. Aside from the giant worm-thing, there seemed to be almost no wild life stirring in the forest, and the normal silence among the trees was beginning to feel ominous. It was like the unearthly stillness before a storm—when the whole of nature seems to be holding its breath, waiting for the explosion of violence.

But there was no storm brewing. The sky was

clear and the sun was bright, above the shadowing canopy of leaf-branches. And there was no sign of imminent violence. The aliens were clearly in another part of the forest, and so—Cord hoped—was the Lamprey. So he pushed the ominous feeling away, and also tried hard not to chafe at the fact that the return journey, to where Samella and Jeko were waiting, seemed longer than the outward stage, that morning.

He glanced up, worriedly, noting that the sun was dipping lower as the afternoon began to wane. What if the encounter with the monstrous worm-thing had turned him around somehow, so that since then he and the others had been travelling the wrong route. . . ?

But almost as that chilling thought came to him, he found that his sense of direction had not let him down. Ahead, they could see the swathe of brightness that meant they were coming to the open area, the treeless corridor left by the crash.

They jogged forward happily, Cord's mouth opening to call to Samella. But then they emerged into the sunlight of the clear area—and Cord's mouth stayed open, while no words formed, and no thoughts entered his frozen, stricken brain.

Two backpacks sat in the midst of the clear space, half unpacked, some of their contents strewn around. But that was all.

Samella and Jeko were not there.

"They wouldn't just walk away," Heleth said firmly, when the shock had worn off enough for them to find their voices.

"No chance," Rontal said. "Anyway, where would they go to? And why?"

They turned helplessly to Cord. But by then the young Highlander had overcome his own feelings of helplessness and panic. He was crouching low, slowly and carefully scanning the turf around the two discarded backpacks.

When he straightened up, his gaze was bleak, and a granite harshness was in his voice.

"They were *taken* away," he said. He pointed to the turf at his feet, where the others saw some odd brown smears. "That's blood. Human blood. I'd say some aliens took them by surprise, and took them away after a fight."

"Took the laserifle, too," Rontal said quietly. "Aliens mightn't do that."

"Maybe not," Cord snapped. "Maybe it was the Lamprey. Whoever it was, they've got Samella and Jeko. And we're going after them."

"Cord, they could be *any*where..." Heleth began.

But Cord was not listening. He was making a wide, crouching circle around the backpacks. Then again he straightened, glaring into the forest.

"More blood here," he said. "That gives us a direction. We'll start off keeping about twenty metres apart, and we'll look at every *scrap* of ground along the way, every tree trunk, for more blood spots or any other kind of trail. Let's go."

Shrugging off his backpack, he strode purposefully off towards the trees. The others, dropping their own packs, hurried to take up their positions, twenty metres on either side of him.

Half an hour later, they were still searching.

Cord had found more smears of blood on the turf at two more points, so he knew they were still on the right trail. But now a new problem had come to add itself to the rage and fear that were clawing at his self-control. The afternoon was fading rapidly into evening, and the gloom among the trees was deepening into murky darkness, made more dense by the newly gathering mist.

Yet he moved on, straining his eyes to see the turf on either side of him, refusing to admit that the darkness was impeding him. And he might have gone plodding on, looking for a trail of blood spots, all through the night, if he had not been halted by Heleth's call.

The call was more like a shriek, and it sent icy terror through Cord's veins as he and Rontal sprinted towards her. And even the gathering darkness did not prevent Cord from recognizing what it was, lying at Heleth's feet.

The crumpled, motionless, blood-smeared body of Jeko.

15
Massacre

"It's all right!" Heleth called. "He's alive!"

The words eased some of the shock and rage that were knotting Cord's insides. And so did the sight of the small crumpled form stirring, struggling to lift itself, as Cord and Rontal came up, and knelt beside Jeko.

The boy's face was a mask of blood, the skin savagely gashed in places, eyes swollen half-shut. His tunic was shredded, and his pale upper body was almost a solid mess of livid bruises. And his left arm hung limply, oddly twisted.

But he was alive, and aware, struggling to find the strength to speak. And when he found his voice, his words came as no real surprise to any of the others.

"The Lamprey," Jeko mumbled, through a mouthful of blood. "Didn't even see him . . . wasn't careful enough. . . ."

"Tell it," Rontal growled.

And Jeko, haltingly and weakly, told them what had happened. How the Lamprey had appeared from nowhere, felling Jeko with one stunning blow, and taking the laserifle. And then how the Lamprey had set out, coldly and savagely, to beat Jeko to death.

"Samella got into it," Jeko mumbled. "Tried to grab the gun. Lamprey just knocked her away. So she ran for it. Guess that saved my life."

When Samella had run, the Lamprey had abandoned Jeko, and pursued her, still carrying the rifle. And Jeko, with a broken arm and more than half-unconscious, had staggered to his feet and tried to follow them.

"I heard Samella yell," he said, "so I guess he caught her. But they never came back. And I kinda wandered around awhile, and then I passed out."

Cord leaned forward intently. "Where were they, Jeko, when you heard Samella yell?"

Jeko raised a shaky hand and pointed. "That way, somewhere."

Cord looked, and nodded grimly to himself. Even in the darkness, he could tell that it was the direction he had expected. He rose to his feet, his hand white-knuckled on the haft of his club, and began to move away.

"Where you goin'?" Rontal demanded.

"I'm going after them," Cord said simply.

Heleth stared. "Alone? And at night? Don't be stupid."

"What should I do?" Cord snapped. "Sit here till morning, while Samella's out there somewhere with that madman? I'd be insane myself, before dawn. And I'll go alone, because Jeko needs looking after—we can't leave him here all night."

"And how are you going to follow them," Heleth asked, "in full dark? You won't be able to see a thing!"

Cord stared past her, into the mist and gloom. "It doesn't matter. I think I know where the Lamprey will be heading. So I'll head that way too."

Rontal followed his gaze, and nodded slowly. "Maybe you're right. But s'pose you find them—you goin' to take the Lamprey on alone, like last time?"

"It won't be like last time," Cord said.

The words were spoken quietly, but their tone made Heleth shiver. And that tone, combined with the blaze of fury in Cord's eyes, made the others realize that there was no more point in arguing further. They were, after all, members of gangs who had followed and obeyed their leaders all their lives. So they merely watched in silence as Cord turned away, swiftly vanishing into the deepening night.

"He shouldn't do it," Heleth said despairingly. "He could run into real trouble—not just the Lamprey, but some aliens maybe, even that huge worm..."

"I know," Rontal said, shaking his head. "But I got this feeling that I wouldn't want to be anything that gets in that boy's way, t'night."

An hour later, in the silent depths of the forest night, the only thing that was getting in Cord's way was trees. Above the forest, the night sky was clear and star-filled, but not a glimmer of light seemed to penetrate down into the almost solid blackness. And Cord was moving like a blind man, blundering painfully into tree trunks that he simply could not see—until he had the sense to hold his club before him, to warn him of the invisible barriers.

But he kept moving. Despite the long day's travelling into the forest, his powerful legs seemed tireless, like the pistons of some hard-working machine. And his mind refused to admit that weariness was even possible—just as it refused to let him give way to anxiety and tension, or even to the frustration of having to move more slowly than he wished, in the blinding darkness. He was driven entirely by rage, and a rock-hard determination.

Somewhere ahead, the Lamprey had Samella as his prisoner. Cord felt a cold certainty that the madman had taken Samella with him because he *wanted* Cord to follow. And Cord felt just as certain that he knew where the Lamprey would go.

A beast will return to its lair, he kept thinking. And I know where this beast's lair is.

Earlier, through a narrow gap in the overhanging leaf-branches, he had picked out a particular spot of brightness among the alien stars, and since then he had used it to guide him, to keep him on the right path. So he moved slowly on, groping and stumbling through endless distances of invisible, mist-shrouded trees.

The night wore on, and Cord lost all sense of time, all sense of himself. Part of his mind seemed to switch off, as if going into suspension or a kind of upright sleep. He became even more like a machine, tireless, single-minded, powered only by that cold and furious determination, which did not dwindle or fade as the slow sightless hours went by.

But eventually, after a time that he could not have measured, awareness seeped back into his emptied mind. Staring ahead through reddened eyes, he realized that he was looking at the tree-trunks, standing like tall ghosts among the swirls of mist. He could see again. Dawn had brought a dim grey light back into the forest.

He glanced up. The stars were still visible, and his guiding star was just where it should have been. During those hours of mindless, automatic plodding, he had kept to an almost geometrically straight line, towards his goal.

He felt a small grim satisfaction. Now he could increase his pace again. And the goal could not be far away. He and the others had reached it in half a day, the previous morning—and even with the slow pace forced on him by the darkness, he was sure that he must be nearly there.

Taking a deep breath, he strode forward, still refusing to recognize even the possibility of tiredness. But he had taken only a few strides at the more rapid pace when he came to a sudden halt.

A sound had broken through the early-morning stillness of the forest—a faint, distant sound, on the threshold of hearing, but wholly recognizable.

The savage, catlike howling of the aliens.

Something in the sound drew icy fingers along Cord's spine, lifting the hairs on his neck. Adrenalin poured through him, sweeping weariness and tension away. And then he was running, a steady pounding lope towards the source of the sound.

There was no reason for him to think that the

alien cries had anything to do with the Lamprey or
Samella. But they seemed to be coming from the
right direction. And they brought with them some of
the foreboding that Cord had felt during the march
through the forest the day before. Instinct, intuition, told him that there had been something
terrible in those weird, distant sounds.

That gruelling run lasted half an hour, yet Cord
gritted his teeth, called on all of his youth and
strength, and kept on. When the run ended, the
forest gloom had brightened a little, as an orange
radiance began to spread across the sky, announcing
the sunrise.

And then Cord saw that his intuition had been
correct. The alien cries did have something to do
with the Lamprey. Something terrible.

He also saw that his guess, the night before,
about the Lamprey's destination, had been right.
The alien cries had led him to the spot where the
Lamprey had made his small fire, in the clearing of
the trees' graveyard.

The beast *had* returned to its lair. But it had not
remained hidden there for long.

As he approached the place, Cord slowed, almost unwilling to draw nearer to the stomach-
churning sight. It reminded him of how he had
always imagined the cruel massacre that was one of
the ancient legends of the Highlands, still recounted
around the peat fires of winter. Except that the
crumpled, bleeding bodies sprawled around the clearing, before him, were those of the alien forest
people.

That was when Cord realized, with horror, how

entirely lucky he was—and Jeko—to have faced the
Lamprey in battle, and survived. For those strewn
alien corpses, which numbered three or four dozen,
showed just how formidable a fighting machine the
Lamprey was.

The forest people had clearly attacked in force,
driven by their anger towards all the humans, and
perhaps by greater anger at the Lamprey's desecration
of the trees' graveyard. The madman, of course, had
had the laserifle—and Cord could see the grisly
burns on many of the corpses, caused by that lethal
beam.

But either the rifle's power pack had given out,
or the forest people had attacked in such numbers
that the Lamprey could no longer use the rifle. Cord
could see that the battle had become savage hand-to-
hand combat. The rest of the fallen alien bodies
showed terrible wounds—they were twisted, crushed
and broken by the brutal, skilled power of the
madman's hands.

Cord edged forward, picking his way among the
bodies, feeling the bile rise in his mouth as his boots
squelched repulsively on the blood-sodden turf. He
could feel his heart thundering against his ribs with
tension. But what he feared most, he did not see.
There was no sign of Samella's presence.

But in the middle of the scattering of bodies, he
found the other thing he had been looking for.
Beneath a heap of dead aliens, their huge eyes blank
and lifeless like windows into infinity, he found the
body of the Lamprey.

Or what was left of it.

The forest people must have swarmed over him

like starving rats, Cord thought, so that no matter
how many he killed there were always too many
more. He saw the broken stump of an alien leaf-
weapon, dark with purplish blood, still gripped in
one of the Lamprey's hands. He saw the remains of
the laserifle lying half under the body, twisted and
bent as if it had been used as a club. And then he
tore his gaze away from the remains of the Lamprey,
turning and retching.

The forest people had all been armed with
leaf-weapons. And when the Lamprey had finally
been overwhelmed, and had fallen beneath the weight
of numbers, they had simply hacked and slashed him
to pieces.

Cord backed away, swallowing hard against the
bitter acid in his mouth, and forced himself to make
a thorough search, all through and around that
blood-soaked area. Twenty minutes later, he leaned
against a tree, sweating, feeling slightly relieved.

Samella's corpse was not on that gruesome bat-
tleground. Whether she was alive or dead, the aliens
must have taken her away with them.

But where? And why. . . ?

The possible answer to those questions burst
into his mind with the force of an explosion, and he
almost cried out. His vision blurred, because all he
could see, in his mind's eye, was the image of a
colossal tree, looming like a tower.

Not there, he moaned silently within himself.
Don't take her there. It will destroy her mind. . . .

As the thoughts formed, he was already running. Not a steady lope this time, but a wild sprint,
weaving at frenzied speed among the trees, towards

that other clearing, nearby, where the vast lone tree stood in majestic splendour.

Even before he came in sight of the clearing, he heard the noise that confirmed his fears—the snarling, feline yowls of the forest people.

Somehow, Cord increased his pace. The sound seemed to be coming from the throats of hundreds of the alien beings, and seemed filled with both rage and dread.

And then he burst through the trees on the edge of the clearing, and horror squeezed his heart in a grip of ice.

Something else had also emerged into the open space, on the far side. A titanic, humped shape, like a moving, turf-covered hilltop. The gigantic worm-thing that he and the others had encountered the day before.

He fought to steady himself, and stared around. There were dozens of the forest people, he saw, near the immensity of the great tree. They were backing away, their huge eyes fixed on the vast worm. And as their movement exposed the base of the tree to Cord's gaze, he felt that horror would drive him mad.

He saw Samella, unconscious, or perhaps dead—slumped and sagging. But she was held upright—by the stout ropes that bound her, immovably, to the mighty tree. Bound and held her, as the monstrous worm slithered out across the clearing towards her.

16
Sacrifice

Behind the paralyzing cloud of horror, part of Cord's mind understood. It was a sacrifice. Probably the forest people would have chosen one of themselves, another time, to be tied to the massive trunk, to give a worm-thing something to feed on instead of the tree's vulnerable brain. But this time, the aliens had a different victim. One who allowed them also to continue their revenge on their tree-killing human enemies.

The thought flashed through Cord's mind while he was still trying to free himself from the grip of horror. But then the paralysis fell away, as if by magic. Samella had moved.

It was only a faint, reflex twist of her shoulders, against the ropes. Her eyes were still closed, and she was probably only semi-conscious. Or so Cord hoped—knowing the appalling mental storm that would be battering at her mind, from the brain of the giant tree. But she was *alive*.

And Cord exploded forward like a missile.

The forest people were still watching the immense worm, slithering unhurriedly to its goal. They did not see Cord until he erupted into their midst, roaring a wordless Highland battle cry, swinging his club like a flail. Screeching, the startled aliens scattered before him. Cord plunged past them, and sprinted towards the tree.

Samella was still slumped against the plaited leather rope that held her, unaware of Cord's presence. Wildly, he gripped the rope, and exerted all the power of his back and arms. The muscles swelled and knotted, the joints crackled with the strain—but the stout rope resisted. And as Cord continued to heave at the rope, cursing himself for not having a knife as the others had, the alien howling around him changed its tone.

But they were not attacking. They had been shrieking with rage as they saw Cord trying to free their sacrifice, but they had stayed away from the tree. Their howls had risen into shrillness because the gigantic worm-thing had almost reached its goal.

It loomed above Cord, rearing up so that it seemed to blot out the sky. It was only a few metres away, the heavy tentacles hissing like snakes as they slashed and flailed. But for a moment it had paused, in its rapid forward slither, as its senses became aware of the different sort of edible prey that was before it.

Within Cord, the fury that had driven him relentlessly through the forest night simply changed direction. Unhesitatingly, he flung himself forward, club swinging, towards those venomous barbs.

There was no plan or idea in his mind for battling the monster. There was nothing in his mind but the single, almost berserk determination—that the ghastly creature should not reach Samella. Not while he was alive.

The club swung, slamming explosively against one of the whipping tentacles. Then Cord dodged aside, as another tentacle slashed down at him, and struck again. After both those ferocious blows, two tentacles hung limp, like broken cables.

But the monster seemed untroubled, and there seemed to be dozens more tentacles. Again Cord dodged and sidestepped, drawing the monster after him, leading it away from the tree, and Samella. For a moment he had to backpedal swiftly, as the monster lunged forward in a sudden slithering rush, with the same terrifying speed that it had shown in the forest. But even as he moved away, Cord swung his club again, furiously, to leave another tentacle useless.

The vast worm's charge halted, and for a moment it reared up even higher, as if studying its enemy. And in that time some of the red mists of fury cleared from Cord's mind. He became dimly aware that he had begun a fight that he could not hope to win. One human with a club could not defeat the monster—could not even hope to damage it seriously. Nor could he turn and run, for the monster's speed was too great. It would catch him within a short distance. Or, worse, it would turn back to the helpless Samella.

Again the giant worm lunged forward. Again Cord dodged away, moving back, the club lashing out at a tentacle. But this time the blow missed—

and the poisoned barb sliced through the air only centimetres from his face.

He backpedalled again, swiftly. As he did so, he became vaguely aware that the exertions of the day and the night before had taken their toll. His weary legs were no longer responding with their usual speed and agility. As he backed away still farther, he knew with a cold sureness that the battle would have to end soon.

Yet the monster was still slithering forward, lunging at him. And a clear memory came into his mind. Rontal, in the forest the day before, leading this same monster into a narrow gap between two trees, where it nearly became solidly wedged. It was a small hope, but the only one he had.

Once again he moved back, evading the lashing tentacles, striking out with the club, which seemed to be growing heavier as his weariness mounted. But the edge of the clearing could not be far away, he thought. And maybe, before his strength gave out, he could find another place where the giant worm might wedge itself—perhaps long enough for him to try again to free Samella.

As he continued his slow, watchful retreat from the worm's furious lunges, he was scarcely aware of the eerie silence around him. The worm attacked soundlessly, save for the whistling lash of the tentacles. Even the cries of the forest beings had faded, as they watched, fascinated, the unequal combat. And in that silence, Cord heard a low, agonized moan, from Samella.

It came just as the worm was charging once again. And it was enough to break the ferocity of his concentration. A tentacle struck at him, and he swung his club too late. The heavy club-head did not collide with the tentacle, but with the lethally sharp hook at its end.

The barb stuck fast in the wood—just as the tentacle jerked back and away. And that powerful jerk ripped the club from Cord's hand, and dragged him off-balance.

He stumbled, and fell, totally exposed.

The next fraction of a second seemed to pass in a terrifying slow motion. The writhing bulk of a tentacle seemed to drift through the air, as it drove furiously down at him. And he seemed unable to move, as in a nightmare. He could only watch, helplessly, as the venomous hook struck down to end his life.

But then something else, which he hardly recognized, flashed through the air over his head. Something that glinted like bright metal. Something sharp, which suddenly blocked the downward slash of the hook, biting deep into the thick flesh of the tentacle.

Then Cord regained his senses, and rolled quickly away to safety, getting to his feet, scarcely able to believe his eyes.

Heleth and Rontal had leaped past him, to take up the battle.

They seemed fresh and unweary, moving like two athletic shadows. Spears in one hand and crude knives in the other, they weaved and dodged away from the stabbing hooks, slashing at the tentacles. And once again the monstrous worm halted its slithering rushes, rearing up as if to take stock of the new development.

Rontal and Heleth backed slowly away, towards Cord. "We can't keep this up for long," Heleth said quickly. "Go help Jeko, Cord, and let's make a run for it."

"Jeko?" Cord repeated blankly, and turned.

The small Streeter was by the tree, next to Samella. He was swathed in bandages, with one arm bound tightly to his side—but with his other hand he was sawing vigorously with his knife at the rope that bound Samella.

Cord went to join him, as quickly as his aching legs would carry him. Behind him he heard a raging yell from Heleth, and looked back to see that the monster had charged once again. Its speed and power seemed unaffected by the few wounds to its tentacles—and Heleth and Rontal were leaping away, striking out desperately with their spears.

But then Cord had reached the tree, in time to help Jeko catch the slumping Samella, and lower her gently to the turf. He saw that Jeko's face was white, deeply etched with lines of pain. But even so, the boy managed to find the ghost of a jaunty grin.

"We got trouble," he said wryly. "That worm's gonna keep after us—and even if it doesn't, the aliens will."

Cord glanced to the side, surprised to realize that he had almost forgotten about the forest beings. They had still not approached the tree, or the furious battle. But they were standing in a menacing huddle, staring at the three humans near the base of the great tree. And they were growling and muttering among themselves, the leaf-weapons glittering in their hands.

Again Cord heard Heleth cry out, and jerked his head around. It seemed that the two warriors had tried to slip around the charging worm, to attack it from the side. But its armoured shell resisted their spears—and before they could seek out the vulnerable joints between the segments of the shell, the whipping tentacles had driven them back once more.

"If we could only kill that thing," Cord said, half to himself, "the aliens might let us go."

"Maybe," Jeko said. He slumped to the turf beside Samella, as if the last of his strength had given out. "Wish we had the laserifle. Or longer spears."

Cord nodded vaguely. And then Jeko's words struck home—and the idea arrived like a sunburst.

He knelt swiftly on the turf. "Samella!" he shouted. "Wake up! You have to wake up!"

The unconscious girl moaned slightly, and stirred. But her eyes did not open. In rough desperation, Cord shook her, and she moaned again. He shook her again, and with a terrible slowness her eyes flickered and half-opened. But they were blank and empty, like mirrors reflecting the monstrous torment within her mind, from the mental power of the mighty tree.

"Samella!" Cord shouted again, still shaking her. "You can *save* us! I know it hurts, but you have to listen!"

Again her eyelids flickered, and hope sprang up within Cord. Awareness was coming back into Samella's gaze. Despite her agony, she was rallying all her inner toughness and control, trying to respond.

"Listen!" Cord begged her. "Hear what I say, and *think*, Samella! Make a picture in your mind!"

He spoke quickly. And the awareness remained in Samella's eyes, though her face was twisting and her body writhing with anguish. For a long, intense moment, when he had finished speaking, Cord stared at her, willing her to succeed. The moment seemed to last a century. And at the end of it Samella sagged, her eyes fluttering shut, sliding back down into a pain-free unconsciousness.

Jeko and Cord looked at each other helplessly. Then they looked around. The fearsome battle was still going on—now some fifty metres away, near the edge of the clearing, as the monstrous worm relentlessly pursued its two enemies. And Heleth and Rontal were tiring. Even as Cord looked, he saw Heleth stumble on the uneven turf—and only a last-minute, agile twist of her hips and backwards leap saved her from the poisoned barb that flashed past her.

And, from the other direction, the aliens were advancing. Slowly but menacingly, the huddle of heavy, dark-furred bodies moved towards the tree, leaf-weapons raised.

Cord found that he had got to his feet, fists clenched. And even Jeko, weak and exhausted as he was, had struggled up, gripping his knife.

He glanced over at Cord, again with the shadow of a grin. "Nice try, anyway, fell'," he said easily. "Like we say in Limbo—only straight folk get to grow old."

Then they turned, and braced themselves for the alien charge.

But the aliens, astonishingly, had halted. Most

of them were staring upwards, awed and silent, at the great tree. A few were turning around, peering back into the forest.

And then Cord heard the sound. Like a faint, distant thunder—or a muffled roll of heavy drums—or a stampede of frightened animals.

He stood motionless, hardly breathing, not daring to hope. And then the stampede erupted out of the forest, into the clearing.

More of the aliens, perhaps a hundred of them. Running at full speed, huge eyes glittering, surging across the open space like a black-furred tide.

But they were not running towards the tree. They were heading for the scene of the monstrous battle, where Rontal and Heleth were still desperately avoiding the giant worm's murderous lunges.

And these aliens did not have the blade-sharp leaf-weapons in their hands. Instead, they carried long poles, with the ends sharpened into crude but effective points.

Cord's yell rang out across the cleraing—a cry of sheer exultation.

"It worked! Samella—*you did it!*"

Despite the great tree's mental power battering against her inner being, Samella had somehow made the picture in her mind, as Cord had asked her to. And the mighty tree had seen that picture, telepathically, and understood, and reached out with its mind to summon the forest beings.

As Rontal and Heleth fell back, astonished and fearful, the hundred aliens rushed howling towards the monstrous worm, the long poles jutting forward like lances.

Cord could hear a hundred sickening, fleshy thuds, as the poles' sharp points struck home. They drove upwards into the ghastly, gaping mouth. They stabbed deep into the crevices between the segments of thick shell. And though the poisoned tentacles slashed and flailed, they were not long enough. They struck only the sturdy poles, unable to reach the aliens who wielded them.

One or two of the poles splintered, but the others held firm. The worm lunged forward furiously, but the lunge only managed to sink the sharpened wood deeper into its flesh. It tried to rear up, to pull away from the hundred stabbing thrusts—but the aliens surged forward, heaving their weight against the poles.

Again the monster lunged at them. But now its movement was slower, weaker. And the aliens saw it, and their voices erupted in a feral screeching howl of triumph. With that cry, they poured all their strength into a final, unstoppable thrust.

The poles sank deeper into the grisly flesh. One or two aliens moved too near, and were flung away in convulsions as deadly flailing barbs found them. But by then the monstrous worm was also in convulsions. The giant body flexed and writhed as it tried to break away from the sharp points that had transfixed it. But the movements were still growing weaker, as its colourless slimy blood gushed like waterfalls from a hundred wounds. Again it tried to rear up, but this time it failed. The vast body began to sag, the tendrils drooped, the cavernous mouth gaped wide.

And then Rontal and Heleth took three light, swift strides forward, and hurled their spears like javelins, with accuracy and furious power, into the glistening centre of that gaping mouth.

The gigantic body seemed almost to fold itself in two, in a final convulsive spasm. And then the monster collapsed, crashing to the ground, where it lay motionless, the tentacles sprawled and limp.

The aliens shrilled with joy at the fall of their terrible enemy. Continuing to stab savagely at the gigantic corpse, they did not seem to notice when Rontal and Heleth drew back, turning to jog wearily towards the tree. Nor did the first group of aliens, that Cord and Jeko had faced, pay any attention to the humans as they rushed to join their fellows in the celebration of victory.

Suddenly exhaustion swept over Cord. He was dimly aware that Jeko had again slumped to the ground, perhaps having fainted from his own weariness and pain. And Cord allowed himself to sag to his knees, next to Samella—to find that she was sitting up, both eyes open and brimming with tears. Yet she was smiling, as if with the purest joy.

Out of the crushing fatigue and release of tension that was numbing his mind, Cord found his voice. "You're . . . all right . . ." he croaked.

"It's the tree!" Samella cried delightedly. "All the trees! They're pouring out their relief, and happiness! It's wonderful, Cord—I wish you could feel it!"

"Maybe I can—a little," Cord said. But then a wave of soothing darkness swept over his mind like the drawing of heavy curtains, and he toppled forward, face down on to the cushioning turf.

17
Klydoreans

"What we don't wanna do," Jeko was saying with a grin, "is strain ourselves. Old Cord here, he stays up all night, gets into a little fight, he just faints away."

Then he ducked, laughing, as Cord pretended to swing a fist at him.

"I've not fainted in my life," Cord said sternly. "I just fell asleep, back there."

"Sure," Rontal drawled. "Everythin' was so quiet and peaceful I nearly dropped off myself."

The laughter rang out in the bright, sunlit air. And Cord sat back, feeling warm and peaceful and immensely happy—as he had been feeling for the previous four very special days.

During those days they had travelled slowly back to where they had left their possessions, and had found all five backpacks just where they had been left, unharmed. They had paused there for a day, to rest and recover, and then had moved on—

still travelling slowly, for Jeko remained weak from his injuries, and Samella was shaky from her own terrible ordeal. But Jeko was healing swiftly, and Samella's skin now hardly showed the bruises left by the Lamprey, as he had dragged her through the forest to his lair, or by the aliens as they had taken her brutally away to be their human sacrifice. And so they had all travelled more cheerfully, and in better spirits, than Cord would once have believed possible.

And now, on the fourth day, they had finally emerged from the forest.

Before them, they saw a broad sweep of plain, covered with the same turf as on the forest floor. The land sloped gently down, towards an immense valley. Cord could see stretches of dark-green that looked like foliage, and a glinting, winding, silvery ribbon that had to be a river and, in the far distance, a smudge of bluish darkness that might be a range of hills, or mountains. To Cord, at that moment, it was the most beautiful landscape he had ever seen.

In fact, he thought, everything is just about perfect. All five of them were alive and safe. They had won a victory over a monstrous, deadly enemy. And they were bound together now, unshakeably, in the closeness of a total friendship.

If it needed proving, that friendship had been proved by the miraculous arrival of Heleth and the Streeters, during Cord's fight with the monster. They told Cord afterwards that, the previous night, they had cleaned Jeko up and bandaged him, and had rested an hour or two, but anxiously and fretfully. And it had been Jeko who had insisted that he was able to travel—and that they could not let Cord face the Lamprey, as they thought, on his own.

So they had set off into the night, towards the graveyard of trees where the Lamprey had had his lair. And they had travelled far more swiftly and directly than Cord—because they were led by the uncanny night vision of the girl from the Bunkers, for whom near-total darkness was no barrier.

So, in the end, they had fought together, and won, and were now even more together than before— which was the main source of Cord's happiness.

"But Jeko is right," Samella was saying. "There's no need to wear ourselves out. We can just wander along, take our time."

"Sure," Jeko said. "Wander along. Climb a few mountains, swim a few oceans. Right, GUIDE?"

They all looked at Samella's backpack, which held the compact computer, fully operative on its solar batteries.

"Klydor has no oceans," GUIDE said softly, "merely some large bodies of fresh water..."

"We know, we know," Jeko broke in. "We heard all that."

"You'll probably hear it again," Samella told him firmly. "GUIDE may not have all his memory banks, but we need whatever he *does* have about Klydor."

Heleth sighed dramatically. "We need lots of things. You sure we shouldn't just stay here?"

Rontal grinned. "In the nice dark forest, outa the sun..."

"Why not?" Heleth demanded. "The Lamprey's dead—and buried, what was left of him—and the aliens and the trees don't hate us any more."

"They don't exactly like us, either," Samella replied. "We're still intruders, and a lot of them are dead because of us. They may be leaving us alone, but they'll be glad to get rid of us."

"You'd think they'd be grateful," Heleth snapped. "We showed them how the bigger worms could be killed."

"And you'd think they coulda thought of it themselves," Jeko put in.

Samella shook her head. "I've told you. They got those poles from the trees' graveyard. They were the *bodies* of young trees—and trees are sacred to the aliens. They would never have used the poles as weapons—not till the biggest tree told them to. Or gave them permission."

Rontal grunted. "We been through all this before. Heleth, you *know* we gotta leave. And me, I wanta see what's out there, away from these brainy trees. So let's get wanderin'."

Cord had said nothing through all this, so when he spoke the others were almost startled—even more by the look in his eyes. A look of resolve, and yet a faraway, dreamy, eager look.

"We're not just going to wander," Cord said. "We have a *goal*. We'll look for a place to live, where we can make our home. We're here to stay—and I want us to claim this world, as *our* world, and make something of it." His eyes shone as he warmed to his theme. "We can have good lives here, just the way we want them. We, us, no one else. No one telling us what to do, how to live, like they do on Earth. For us, it's a free world—*our* world."

A moment of thoughtful silence followed, broken at last by Rontal. "Could be other aliens, Cord. Their world first."

Cord shrugged. "There'll be room for us, without troubling any other beings. It's a big world. There'd be room here for all the kids in Limbo, or the Bunkers, and more. If we had a way to get them here."

Jeko laughed. "That'd be a thing. Scoop them up from under the CeeDee noses and bring them to live in a nice free world."

But Samella wasn't smiling. "Cord, you haven't mentioned the one thing that will finish that dream of yours before it starts. ColSec. Remember there's an inspection team coming, in six months, to check on us *colonists.*"

"Right," said Heleth sullenly. "What happens to our 'free world' then? Whatever we do, it'll be a colony, where ColSec can come and start pushing us around."

The others muttered their agreement, as Cord stared round at them. And he, too, knew that what Heleth said was true. But her words had also served to reawaken the small, hard flame that had been born within him even before the shuttle had crashed. The flame of anger and hatred, for ColSec.

"*No!*" he said.

The others tensed, jolted by the flinty rage in his eyes and voice.

"ColSec sent us here not caring if we lived or died," Cord went on. "But we've lived. And we'll go on living, our own free lives. Whatever we have to do."

"Like take on ColSec?" Rontal asked, pointedly.

"ColSec is on Earth," Cord replied, "and this is Klydor. So they'll send an inspection team. We'll just have to be ready for them. We have to be ready for *anything*—if we think our freedom, our world, is worth fighting for."

He stared around at the others. Rontal was nodding gravely. Heleth was looking uneasy, but she too nodded as she met Cord's eyes. Samella gave him a crooked grin of total agreement. And Jeko, inevitably, laughed.

"We'll just bring that inspection team back here," he said, "and let 'em inspect the inside of another big worm."

Then they were all smiling at each other, and especially at Cord. And his answering grin held all the wild courage, the granite stubbornness, the unbending will, that had been handed down over hundreds of years by his Highland ancestors.

He rose to his feet, reaching a brawny arm to scoop up his backpack. "All right, you Klydoreans," he said, the fierce grin widening. "Let's go and look at our world."

ABOUT THE AUTHOR

Douglas Hill was raised in the backwoods of Canada in Prince Albert, Saskatchawan. "Its main claim to fame," he says, "is that it's the second coldest town in North America." The landscape of his childhood was one of vast plains and forests, snow-covered in winter but full of blazing sunshine in summer. "The backwoods of Canada were a great place to grow up in but a lousy place to be an adolescent." Douglas Hill says, "I was a dreamer. I devoured science fiction. Flash Gordon and Buck Rogers were major comic strips in the newspapers in those days, and I read every one." He left home at age seventeen to attend university, first in Saskatoon and then moving east to school in Toronto. At age twenty-three, he moved east again—to England. In 1963, Douglas Hill began reviewing science fiction for the London weekly, *Tribune*. He was for some years Literary and Arts editor of *Tribune*, but now spends his time writing and advising publishers. His books include The Last Legionary series, four books about Keill Randor, and *Young Legionary*, Keill's early adventures, as well as The Huntsman trilogy.

Coming in August . . .
Volume Two in
The Colsec Trilogy

The Caves of Klydor

by Douglas Hill

With limited supplies and only the weapons they had
made, the five exiles explore Klydor, searching for a place
to build a colony. But their search for a home takes them
into the heart of a new battle for survival, which also has
at stake the continuation of a rebel uprising against the
Organization.

Read THE CAVES OF KLYDOR, on sale August 15,
1986 wherever Bantam Spectra Books are sold.

BANTAM
SHOP·AT·HOME
C·A·T·A·L·O·G

Special Offer
Buy a Bantam Book
for only 50¢.

Now you can have an up-to-date listing of Bantam's hundreds of titles plus take advantage of our unique and exciting bonus book offer. A special offer which gives you the opportunity to purchase a Bantam book for only 50¢. Here's how!

By ordering any five books at the regular price per order, you can also choose any other single book listed (up to a $4.95 value) for just 50¢. Some restrictions do apply, but for further details why not send for Bantam's listing of titles today!

Just send us your name and address and we will send you a catalog!